From the Desk of Alexis Mosley,
Wedding Planner

Today's To-Do List

1. Feed the cat.

2. Confirm floral delivery for tomorrow's wedding.

3. Check with Kinley Carmichael re: seating arrangements for reception. Look surprised when her brother Logan appears.

4. Check with Logan re: lighting for garden ceremony. Act as if we barely know each other.

5. Make sure house is clean before Logan comes over tonight.

6. Have an evening of amour with Logan. Pretend it doesn't mean anything.

7. Do not, under any circumstances, fall in love!

Bride Mountain:
Where a walk down the aisle is never far away...

HEALED WITH A KISS

BY
GINA WILKINS

Published in Great Britain 2014
by Mills & Boon, an imprint of Harlequin (UK) Limited,
Eton House, 18-24 Paradise Road, Richmond, Surrey, TW9 1SR

© 2014 Gina Wilkins

ISBN: 978 0 263 91287 6

23-0514

Gina Wilkins is a bestselling and award-winning author who has written more than seventy novels. She credits her successful career in romance to her long, happy marriage and her three "extraordinary" children.

A lifelong resident of central Arkansas, Ms Wilkins sold her first book to Mills & Boon in 1987 and has been writing full-time since. She has appeared on the Waldenbooks, B. Dalton and *USA TODAY* bestseller lists. She is a three-time recipient of a Maggie Award for Excellence, sponsored by Georgia Romance Writers, and has won several awards from the reviewers of *RT Book Reviews*.

For my Izzie, who is always curled beside me
to keep me company while I write.

Chapter One

Alexis Mosley stood toe to toe with innkeeper Logan Carmichael, not at all intimidated by his dark scowl. "I don't think my client is asking that much of you, really," she said coolly. "Can you provide the services she wants or not?"

"Your client," he retorted with a deep line carved between his straight, dark eyebrows, "needs to get a grip on reality. This is Southwest Virginia, not Montego Bay. If she wants a Jamaican beach wedding, she should hold it there. Or at the least make the five-hour drive to Virginia Beach and get married where there's an actual ocean."

Alexis sighed gustily. "As I've already explained to you, she needs to have the wedding here because she has elderly family members in very poor health who can't travel easily but want to see her married. She's dreamed of a Montego Bay wedding because that's where her fiancé proposed two years ago. That isn't possible for them this year, so she wants to move up her wedding date to July and re-create the feel here."

On this Monday morning in early March, Alexis was consulting with Logan and his two sisters, Kinley and Bonnie, co-owners of Bride Mountain Inn, to determine whether her client's very specific and somewhat unconventional requests were within reason. According to Logan, they were not.

With a sardonic expression on his sternly attractive face, he made a slow turn, motioning with one hand to draw her attention to the tidy garden in which they stood, the Queen Anne–style bed-and-breakfast behind them, the white gazebo at the end of a pebbled path. A tall, three-tiered fountain reigned in the center of the still-winter-dormant garden, providing the rhythmic splash of falling water for a soothing sound track. Against the horizon, the majestic Blue Ridge Mountains rose proudly against the pale blue sky. He had a point about the setting looking very little like a Jamaican beach.

Kinley, predictably enough, jumped into the discussion to state differently. "Of course we can make your client happy! It won't be the first tropical-themed wedding we've held here. We'll just have to figure out a way to set up to her personal specifications. I'm sure among all of us, we can come up with something."

While Logan's reaction to over-the-top bridal desires was often negative, inveterate saleswoman Kinley's was just the opposite. To book an event at the inn, she seemed willing to promise just about anything— and yet, surprisingly, she always came through, proving she agreed only to what she knew they could accomplish.

In almost a year of working with the Carmichael siblings through her event-planning business, Alexis had never registered a complaint after an event at Bride Mountain Inn. She recommended the inn frequently as a venue for the weddings and other special occasions she coordinated. And nearly every time, she ended up wrangling with Logan at some point over the outdoor setups, more than once being told her requests were impossible even though they both knew that somehow he would make it work.

"Have your client consult with you on a very detailed list of her ideas, then we'll all get together and discuss them," Kinley instructed. "Make sure she knows all her decisions have to be made in time for us to make arrangements, and she can't have last-minute changes with a theme this specific. We'll do our best to make her happy."

Alexis understood Kinley's need to have everything spelled out in advance to avoid complications later. She operated her own business on exactly the same philosophy. "I'll explain it to her, of course."

"I'll research some Jamaican recipes in case she wants us to provide special breakfasts or snacks for her guests," Bonnie contributed, looking intrigued by the challenge. "I'm sure there are many more original ideas than jerk chicken."

The siblings didn't look particularly alike. Kinley had a slender, fit body, brown hair streaked with honey highlights and grayish-blue eyes. Bonnie was petite, with golden-blond curls and big blue eyes. Older brother Logan was hard-carved, medium tall and muscular, with dark hair and hazel eyes. Alexis wouldn't call him handsome, exactly, but definitely the type of man any red-blooded woman would notice. She'd definitely noticed the first time she'd met him.

Logan blew out a resigned breath that hung just visible in the crisp morning air. The fleece-lined gray jacket he wore with a T-shirt, jeans and boots was his only concession to the chilly temperature. He would ditch the jacket when the days warmed, but the rest of his outfit remained the same year-round, at least from Alexis's observation.

"Just give me and the crew time to work whatever miracle you think I can pull off. You find the stuff she wants, I'll set it up. But you're not hauling in sand," he added with a warning scowl. He shot a dark look at Kinley before continuing, "Last time someone had the clever idea of setting up sandboxes for the kids at a tropical theme party, I had a hell of a time cleaning up afterward."

"No sand," Alexis promised.

He held her gaze for a moment, then nodded, turned and walked away with a mumble about needing to get back to work. His gait was marked by a very slight limp on the left side, which was more intriguing than detracting. As he disappeared around the side of the inn, Alexis made herself stop looking after him and spoke to his sisters. "I'll try to keep the bride realistic with her expectations."

"I know you will," Kinley said with a smile. "Don't mind Logan, he's just grouchy today. He and his crew are working long hours to get the grounds ready for spring plantings."

Alexis couldn't help laughing. "He's grouchy *today?*"

Kinley smiled a bit sheepishly, while Bonnie grinned in acknowledgment that their brother wasn't the jolliest soul even on the best of days. Logan wasn't a jerk, Alexis mused. He was just bluntly candid and impatient with most social niceties. And yet during the past year she had seen him interacting kindly with children and senior citizens, politely if somewhat distantly with stressed-out brides and nervous grooms, and relaxed and easy with his small, hardworking, fiercely loyal grounds crew. She wouldn't say he was all bark and no bite, exactly—he wasn't quite that innocuous—but she'd worked with worse.

As different as the Carmichael siblings were, they meshed amazingly well. They worked together every day at the inn they'd inherited from a great-uncle and had restored and reopened for business. Bonnie and Logan even lived full-time on the grounds; Bonnie in a two-bedroom, half-basement apartment; Logan in a cozy caretaker's cottage downhill from the wedding gazebo. Alexis figured she would have long since strangled her younger brother, Sean, if they tried to go into business together.

Kinley and Bonnie had both married during the past winter, since Alexis had first started working with them. Yet bringing new members into the fold had not seemed to affect the family dynamics, at least when it came to the interactions she had witnessed. She enjoyed watching the sisters and brother work together, putting their individual strengths into results that were always impressive.

She was quite sure it would be interesting, as usual, to work with them on this newest project. She even looked forward to more spirited skirmishes with Logan, which always added a nice bit of spice to her workdays.

Darkness had fallen that evening when Alexis brewed a cup of hot tea in her cozy kitchen, only a few miles from Bride Mountain Inn. The days were getting a little longer as spring drew nearer. Already her work hours were increasingly busy with preparations for May and June, the craziest time of year in the wedding business. She wasn't complaining about the workload. Having acquired Blue Ridge Celebrations just over a year ago, she was pleased to have seen a marked increase in bookings during the past months. She'd invested wisely in advertising, and had worked hard to make sure word-of-mouth endorsements from her clients were nothing but positive.

For some reason, she found herself thinking back over the past as she carried her tea into the living room with her affectionate gray cat, Fiona, padding along beside her. Though she'd trained for a career in music and theater, she had worked in her mom's Roanoke, Virginia, florist shop during her school years and later in shops in Maryland and New York, so she'd been quite familiar with weddings and other fancy events. She had always displayed a talent for event planning, enjoying that part of her jobs with florists. She'd spent quite a bit of time developing that skill during what had been supposed to be only supplemental work.

A few months after her twenty-seventh birthday she'd acknowledged that she lacked the all-consuming passion required to become a major star on stage. She'd loved performing, and she'd worked very hard at perfecting her skills, but the lack of control over her own future had become more and more difficult to accept. After being passed over for an important role she'd come so close to obtaining—and coming to the abrupt realization that she wasn't devastated by the rejection—she had found the courage to change her life course and go into business for herself.

It hadn't been easy to turn her back on the goal she'd had for so long. She'd walked away from her friends, her tiny but adorable city apartment and a tumultuous relationship that had left her ego bruised and her heart barricaded. It had been a terrifying, but ultimately liberating, move.

Drawn back to her home state, she had purchased this established enterprise almost an hour's drive from her mother's still-thriving florist shop. Her natural talent for organization and creative thinking had come in handy in her new career, and she'd had considerable help from the previous owner and from a couple of employees who'd stayed with the company after the transfer.

There had been a few glitches initially, a few minor missteps, but all in all Alexis was satisfied she'd made the right decision, despite her enthusiastic stage mother's disappointment and concern. Now twenty-nine, she was independent and self-sufficient; she had established functional and strictly enforced boundaries with her family; she had a nice rented house she was considering buying, and several good friends. She even enjoyed a nondemanding, drama-free but physically exciting connection with a fascinating man who was no more interested than she was in the challenges of long-term romantic commitments. What more could a modern-day woman want?

As if to accompany that thought, a brisk tap on the front door got her attention just as she set her steaming cup of tea on the low table in front of the couch. Along with the knock came a scrabbling sound on the front porch that she recognized easily enough.

"Sounds as though we both have company," she said to her cat, who stared at the door with eagerly perked ears. "They're a little early. Think they were impatient to see us?"

She smoothed her hands over the pink knit top and faded jeans she'd changed into after arriving home from work only an hour earlier. Her dark hair hung loose around her shoulders, but she merely shook it back rather than fussing with it. She was barefoot, but didn't bother donning shoes as she moved across the room. It was nice to know she could be entirely herself with this particular visitor, whom she had been expecting tonight. Already her pulse had increased in pleasurable anticipation as she reached to open the door.

Logan Carmichael stood on her doorstep, his characteristically stern face illuminated by the yellow bulb in her porch light fixture. Beside him, a massive black-and-brown dog made a husky, deep-chested sound that some might have interpreted as a growl.

Logan jerked his chin toward the rottweiler-mix dog. "He begged to come with me tonight. He sulked that I left him home the last couple of times. Hope it's okay."

Smiling, Alexis moved back out of the doorway. She knew quite well the dog's grumbly rumble was merely his unique way of greeting people he liked, his own version of a cat's purr. "Ninja is always welcome here," she said, motioning for them to come inside. "Fiona, you have a visitor."

Ninja headed straight for the gray cat, who leaped onto the couch to better greet the big dog. Alexis was no longer even bemused when her pet rubbed affectionately against Ninja's head, triggering a new spate of rumbling from the dog's broad chest and a frantic wagging of his tail. Someone had forgotten to tell the silly creatures that they were supposed to be sworn enemies. They had become great pals instead over the past five months. Odd, yes, but Alexis figured it was no more surprising than her own very private friendship with Logan.

Logan closed the door, shrugged out of his jacket and tossed it over a chair. He reached out then to wrap his hand around the back of her head and tug her closer, his hazel eyes glinting with a rare, slow smile. "Is Ninja the only one welcome here?"

She rested her right hand on his solid chest, feeling his heart beating a bit rapidly beneath her palm and relishing the knowledge that she elicited that response from him. Slipping off her glasses with her left hand, she smiled up at him through her lashes, openly flirting, comfortable with touching him and yet highly stimulated by the contact. "I suppose it's okay if you accompany him occasionally."

He chuckled, his warm breath brushing her lips as he lowered his head. "I appreciate that gracious invitation," he said, just before taking her mouth in a hungry kiss that effectively changed their banter into passion.

She didn't bother to ask him to take a seat, or to po-

litely offer refreshments. Instead, when the long, thor-
ough kiss finally broke off, she moved a step back and
took his hand. Turning, she led him to her bedroom,
a path he knew well already, having visited there an
average of three times a month since late October.

She didn't turn on the overhead light. The stained-
glass lamp beside her antique four-poster bed was
on, the dimmed light filtered through red, purple and
gold tinted glass. The white duvet was already turned
back to reveal white sheets and soft, fluffy pillows.
She had considered lighting one or more of the thick
white candles scattered around the room, but she'd
decided not to. She and Logan had a mutually satisfying relationship uncluttered by the traditional and
potentially painful trappings of "romance." They were
friends. Good friends. Friends with benefits, in somewhat dated slang. But neither had expectations for a
permanent commitment.

Which didn't mean she couldn't enjoy every minute with him while it lasted, she thought, melting into
his work-toned arms.

Their lovemaking began slowly, both taking their
time as they shed clothing and caressed the skin revealed. Alexis never tired of tracing his impressive
abs and biceps with her fingertips and lips. Despite
the old scars on his left leg that he had attributed without elaboration to an old college injury, Logan was in
the best physical condition of anyone she knew. Solid,
strong, tanned and fit, a combination of hard work and
healthy living. And, oh, did he know how to put that
amazing body to good use.

They communicated with appreciative murmurs
and throaty sighs, with soft laughter and quiet moans.

As had happened each time before, the kisses and embraces rapidly escalated into a desperate need that made it impossible for them to take their time and savor. The tidy bedclothes were tangled, shoved aside, pillows tossed to the floor.

Logan donned protection swiftly, then returned to her. Clearing her mind of any thoughts but that moment, she welcomed him eagerly.

It took quite a while for Logan to decide that his limbs would support him if he tried to rise. Some ten minutes after he and Alexis had reached explosive orgasms, he lay on his back in her tumbled bed, his breathing still a little ragged, his heart rate just returning to a somewhat steady rhythm. How could it keep getting better with her, when each time he was convinced he'd never felt that good before?

Alexis lay against his side, so still and quiet he wasn't even certain she was awake. He slanted a glance down at her, but her hair fell over her face, hiding her eyes. He would tuck it back for her, but he wasn't sure he could move his arm yet.

She sighed then and raised her head. The diffused glow from the stained-glass lamp glinted in her dark brown hair when she shoved it back with a slightly unsteady hand. Her smoke-gray eyes reflected the multicolored light. Her cheeks were a little flushed, and her full lips were still darkened from his kisses. She looked as though she had just had a round of hot, energetic, very satisfying lovemaking. Sex, he corrected himself quickly. Great sex.

He liked seeing her like this, all tousled and sleepy-eyed, so different from the tidy, tailored appearance she presented when on the job. Of course, he liked looking at her then, too, knowing what lay beneath her tastefully modest professional wardrobe, picturing her with her usually pinned-up dark hair tangled around her bare shoulders and remembering the taste of her soft mouth beneath his.

"Wow," she said.

He chuckled. "Seconded."

That was something else he liked about her. She wasn't shy or coy about her enjoyment of sex, though he was aware that she was very selective about satisfying her needs. The first night they were together, she'd admitted that she hadn't been with anyone else recently. He'd replied just as candidly that he'd been in the midst of a dry spell himself, though he hadn't elaborated. It wasn't lack of opportunity that had made him live a rather monklike existence for the past couple of years. He'd simply been very careful not to get involved in any potentially messy entanglements, and he wasn't the type to particularly enjoy a series of one-night stands with strangers.

Alexis had been the first woman in quite a while who'd drawn him out of his self-imposed solitude. In addition to being strongly attracted to her physically, he genuinely liked her. He admired her intelligence, her competence, her quick wit, her directness. She'd told him flat-out that weddings were her business, not her aspiration, and on that they could fervently agree. He had his reasons for being commitment-shy—good reasons, in his opinion. Obviously, Alexis had her own. They didn't discuss their past relationships, but they had a lot in common when it came to what they wanted for now.

No one else knew they were seeing each other. They had agreed there was no need to complicate their easy friendship with outside expectations from friends and family. It was no one else's business, in Logan's opinion. He wasn't seeing anyone else, and neither was Alexis, but they were both free to do so. He simply wasn't interested in dating others at the moment. And he rather hoped she felt the same way. At least for now.

Rising to her elbow, she propped her head on her hand and gazed down at him. "Now that we've gotten that out of the way—"

He laughed softly, amused by her wording.

"—can I get you anything? I made tea for myself, but I suspect it's cold now. I could brew fresh for both of us."

"Sounds good, but I can't stay much longer. Have to get an early start tomorrow working on a raised herb bed Bonnie wants me to put in this year. She had a little garden last year, but she's decided it's too small. Curtis and I are going to start on the bigger one in the morning."

Though he and Alexis didn't talk much about their pasts, they chatted quite a bit about work. She shared funny, just-between-them anecdotes about some of her events, probably because she knew he'd keep her confidences. He told her about the plans his sisters concocted for the inn and its grounds, most of which they expected him to handle, of course. During the past winter, he'd overseen construction of two easily accessible restroom/dressing room facilities beneath the inn's back deck for use by wedding parties and their guests. Kinley and Bonnie had a sizable list of other improvements they wanted to make as time and finances allowed.

It would take several years to complete everything on their list—assuming, of course, they didn't add to it, which they surely would—but he wasn't complaining. All part of the job he'd taken on when he'd agreed to go into business with them. And that didn't even include the part-time software consultation he performed on the side. Kinley maintained her real estate sales license and showed homes to prospective buyers during quite a few of her evenings away from the inn. Neither of them would completely give up their side jobs until they were certain the inn was entirely solvent.

Alexis didn't bother dressing after climbing out of the bed, but wrapped herself in a soft red robe that set off her dark hair and gray eyes quite nicely. While she went to the kitchen to put on the kettle for tea, he washed and dressed again in the jeans and T-shirt he'd worn for this casual visit. He took a moment to straighten the bed before joining her. Even so soon after being thoroughly sated, he felt his blood heat in response to the images that flooded his mind when he smoothed the sheets.

She had the tea ready when he joined her. The earthy scent of chamomile wafted through her kitchen, all stainless steel and white with a few splashes of red as accents. Alexis had decorated primarily with white fabrics, light woods and clear glass, very clean, streamlined and non-fussy. Typical of her, he mused, taking a white-cushioned seat at the glass-topped table.

Ninja wandered into the room and sat at Logan's

feet, looking at Alexis expectantly. With a laugh, she pulled out a doggy treat from her pantry and tossed it to him. Not to be ignored, Fiona wound around Alexis's ankles, meowing until Alexis gave in and slipped her a tuna-flavored kitty snack. It made Logan frown to realize that she had gotten into the habit of having both cat and dog treats on hand, but he brushed off that thought, telling himself it didn't mean anything. He didn't want to ruin the evening by overthinking things.

Setting the tea in front of him, she smiled. "What about you, Logan? Should I toss you a treat? I think I have some cookies."

He shook his head. "I'm good with the tea, thanks."

She took the chair closest to him and lifted her cup to her lips, smiling at him over the rim. Her robe parted a bit with the movement, giving him a fleeting glimpse of creamy breast. He gulped tea fast enough to scald his mouth, then chided himself for acting like a randy teenager around her, even though they had just climbed out of her bed. How did she keep doing that to him, despite his best efforts to remain in complete control around her?

To distract himself, he stuck with the one topic always guaranteed to keep their conversations flowing comfortably. Their work.

"You haven't mentioned how your big wedding went this past weekend," he said, trying to hide the fact that his tongue felt as though he'd burned off a layer.

She groaned heartily at the mention of one of the biggest events she'd coordinated since taking over her business. "It was exhausting. If all my brides were as difficult as that one, I'd get out of the business to-morrow."

He knew the wedding had been held at one of the biggest churches in Southwest Virginia and had been one of the social events of the late-winter season for that particular crowd. There had been a carriage and white horses, doves and chamber musicians, with an obscenely expensive dinner and reception afterward at a nearby country club. Bride Mountain Inn had never even been in the running as a venue for that fancy event, but it sounded to him as though he should be grateful for that. "Did you manage to meet all her demands?"

"She even promised to recommend me to her friends," Alexis replied with a weary but satisfied smile. "And by the way? I give the marriage a year. Maybe two, though that's stretching it."

Logan winced. "Problems getting along?"

"The groom hit on me half an hour before the wedding."

Logan's teacup hit the table with a thump. "He *what?*"

Ninja sat beside Alexis's chair and rested his head on her knee. She rubbed his ears affectionately. Fiona jumped into Logan's lap, as if to prove that she, too, could claim human attention if she desired. Still scowling, Logan absently stroked the cat's back, eliciting a butt-up response that begged for more. "How did he hit on you? Are you sure that's what it was?"

"He caught me in a corner, stood entirely too close and said maybe he and I could get together sometime—to plan an event, he added with a wink. What does that sound like to you?"

"Like he was hitting on you," Logan muttered.

"Thank you."

"You, uh, didn't mention it to the bride, I assume?"

"Of course not. Not only would he have accused me of totally misinterpreting it, making me look like an idiot, but it really wasn't any of my business. Besides, the bride was busy flirting with the cellist in the chamber quartet. Like I said, I give them a year."

Logan shook his head in distaste. "We've had a few of those at the inn—you know, weddings that seem doomed to failure almost from the start. Kind of leaves you with a bad taste in your mouth, doesn't it?"

She nodded. "I much prefer completing a job with at least a modicum of hope that the couple will somehow make it work despite the odds against them."

"High odds," he agreed.

"Very high odds."

Figuring they'd made their point, he let it go at that.

"Did I ever mention my parents were divorced?" she asked nonchalantly, looking down at Ninja. "Twice for my dad. He was married briefly after he and Mom split. He was engaged again when he died of a blood infection two years ago. Mom's third marriage has lasted almost a decade so far, though she and my stepfather sort of go their own ways."

He wasn't quite sure what to say. He'd known her father was dead and her mother remarried, but not the rest. He and Alexis didn't talk about their family lives, though, because she worked often with his sisters, she was somewhat more aware of his. She knew, for example, that his parents had split up when he was just a kid, that he and his sisters had been raised by their single mom in Tennessee, that his mother had died almost five years ago and that his dad was a footloose world traveler who had rarely seen his son and daughters since the divorce. Alexis had even met his father in passing when she'd visited the inn one winter morning for a meeting with Kinley about an upcoming event.

Making the long trip from his latest temporary home in New Zealand, Robert Carmichael had come to Virginia in December to see his daughters married. Arranging their plans around their father's rare visit, Kinley and Bonnie had shared an intimate double wedding in front of the fireplace in the inn parlor with only close family members in attendance.

Logan had told Alexis a little about the wedding when he'd slipped off to visit her the next night, but he'd been careful to avoid any discussion about his emotions at seeing his father for the first time in two years, or any analysis of his feelings about growing up with an absentee dad. Nor had she asked any such personal questions. That wasn't the sort of relationship he had with her, by mutual unspoken agreement.

"My brother's been married twice, too," she said, breaking into his wandering thoughts. "Neither one lasted. He's only twenty-seven."

He was getting a clearer understanding of Alexis's distrust of marriage vows. With her family history, she had good reason to be cynical about those "till death do us part" promises. Had she been met with disappointments of her own that had only reinforced her early, disillusioning experiences? "Started young, didn't he?"

She shrugged. "He's the impulsive type."

"Kinley's first marriage didn't take, but I think

she and Dan have the potential to make it work," he commented, scratching her cat's ears when she head-butted his hand in a less-than-subtle hint. "And Bonnie and Paul have as good a chance as anyone, I think. My sisters are nothing if not determined."

Though his parents had divorced, he'd seen examples of successful lifelong unions—his maternal grandparents, and his great-uncle Leo and great-aunt Helen, who'd been committed to each other until her untimely death. Leo had been faithful to those vows even for the eighteen years he outlived his beloved wife. So Logan knew it was possible for others—he just didn't know if it was for him. His own record of betrayals and disappointments had left him with a romantic cynicism he wasn't sure he could ever overcome, or even wanted to, at this point.

"Your brothers-in-law seem very nice. You like them, don't you?"

"Yeah, they're great guys. We're becoming friends as well as family."

Propping her chin on her hand, she studied him with a faint smile, her tone lightening the mood. "Any concerns about their butting into your business at the inn?"

Even to him, his answering smile felt a little arrogant, which he hadn't exactly intended. But still, he said, "That's not going to happen. For one thing, we made sure both guys signed prenups, making it clear they have no claims on the inn in case the marriages break up."

He'd said "we," but the truth was that he alone had made sure of that precaution. His experience with a less-than-ethical business partner had left him wary of putting his trust in anyone other than his sisters when it came to business, even the likable, upstanding citizens they had married.

"Wise move. But maybe your sisters will make their marriages last. Some people do. And the fact that eternal optimists keep trying means more business for us, huh?" Alexis added with a wink.

He smiled, pleased to be back on comfortable footing, conversationwise. "You've got that right."

It was the most they'd talked about their families in the almost five months since they'd crossed paths at a local coffee shop late one restless autumn evening. They hadn't known each other very well at that point, having met only a few times through their work, but there'd been a strong attraction. They'd struck up a casual, surprisingly enjoyable conversation that had gone on for more than an hour, and he'd ended up following her home after her refreshingly straightforward invitation. Twenty minutes after they'd walked through her front door they'd been in her bed. And it had been the best experience of his life. Until the next time they'd gotten together, anyway. And then the time after that...

He set the cat on the floor, stood and carried his empty teacup to the sink. "I'd better head home. I've got a report to write tonight for a software client."

With one last pat for Ninja, Alexis rose, too. "I'm bringing two clients by the inn later this week to look over the place as a potential venue for events—a wedding next year and a vows renewal ceremony being held in July. The vows couple are celebrating their fortieth wedding anniversary—another pair who've beaten the odds—and they are lucky the inn is avail-

able for a booking that soon if they approve of the setting, which I'm sure they will."

"They're not going to want sand or palm trees, are
they?" he asked with a frown.

Sighing, she shook her head. "I haven't talked specific details with either client yet, but I got the impression the older couple, in particular, wants something
simple and sweet for the recommitment ceremony."

"Good. Wish you'd talk more of your clients into
that theme. Simple and sweet, I mean."

She grinned and reached up to pat his cheek. "And
miss seeing your expressions when I make outrageous
demands of you? You'd be taking away half the fun
of my job."

He grumbled, but couldn't resist brushing a quick
kiss over her smile. "See you around."

"Sure. See ya, Logan."

Very casual. Very civil. Very open-ended. Exactly
the way he liked it, he thought as he and Ninja headed
out to his truck. He held open the driver's-side door
and the dog leaped in gracefully, settling into position
in the passenger's seat, ready to enjoy the ride home.

It didn't take much to make his dog happy. A ride
in the truck. A crunchy treat. A friendly rub from a
pretty lady. All things Logan enjoyed himself. Ninja
didn't dwell on the past or worry about the future.
He just…lived.

After reaching out to pat his buddy's broad head,
Logan fastened his seat belt and started the truck. He
could do a lot worse than to emulate his dog.

Chapter Two

Alexis arrived at Bride Mountain Inn on Thursday afternoon ten minutes earlier than she'd agreed to meet her clients. She parked in the lot in front of the building, noting that few other cars were there. It was off-season in the bed-and-breakfast business in the Blue Ridge Highlands—a little past the peak snow sports time and just a few weeks early for the popular spring and summer outdoor activities. From conversations they'd had during their collaborations, she knew Kinley had been working on ideas for boosting business for next year's off-season. Still, the inn stayed quite busy during peak season and seemed to be performing to the Carmichael siblings' satisfaction thus far.

The gray-sided, white-trimmed inn really was lovely, wearing its years well thanks to the loving care it had received. Multiple gables and windows and roof peaks combined with white gingerbread trim provided traditional Queen Anne charm, while the bright red double entry doors served as a warm, cheery welcome. The wraparound porch that merged onto the back deck was finished with a white post-and-spindle banister and lined with rockers from which to admire the spectacular views of the mountains against the horizon. One middle-aged couple, dressed warmly for the cool afternoon, sat in rockers on the side porch sipping something out of big mugs and engaged in a lively conversation, clearly relishing a day of relaxation.

During the past months, Alexis had learned some of the history of this place from Kinley and Bonnie, who took great pride in their establishment. Built in the 1930s by their great-grandfather, the inn had then been passed down to Leo Finley, great-uncle to Logan and his sisters, who'd operated it with his beloved wife, Helen, until her death. After Helen died, Leo closed the inn to guests and lived alone in the downstairs apartment for the remaining eighteen years of his life. Upon his death, he left the inn to the great-nephew and great-nieces who had visited him often from Tennessee and whom he had loved very much. It had taken them almost a year to have the inn ready for guests again, and they'd invested everything they'd had to do so. Just this past November, they had celebrated their two-year reopening anniversary with a reception for local travel agents, events planners, caterers and other business collaborators. Alexis had attended, and it had been very nice.

She and Logan had barely spoken to each other

during that event. He had participated with almost visible reluctance peeking through his deeply ingrained Southern manners. She suspected his sisters had coerced him into being there. Alexis hadn't stayed long, but she'd enjoyed the reception and had left confident that, though she and Logan had been lovers for almost a month by then, no one else in attendance had suspected they were anything more than cordial business associates. Four months later, no one was any the wiser. She saw no need to discuss their affair with anyone, either now or after its inevitable ending.

Only one person knew about her trysts with Logan—her best friend, Paloma Villarreal. Despite living in different states since Alexis had returned from New York to Virginia to start her new career, she and Paloma had remained in close contact, still sharing secrets during long, candid phone conversations. Paloma had been intrigued to hear that Alexis was seeing someone. Being somewhat of a commitment-phobe herself, she totally understood why her friend was so leery of getting too emotionally involved. She didn't ask too many questions, leaving it up to Alexis to decide how much to share. They respected each other's privacy, a trait Alexis valued highly after growing up with a mother who wasn't big on boundaries.

Alexis's mother, who had no clue about Logan, had spent the past year and a half throwing one single doctor or lawyer after another in her only daughter's direction, pointing out in frustration that Alexis was rapidly approaching thirty without a respectable marriage prospect in sight. No matter how many times Alexis asked her mother to butt out of her social life, her mom still managed to work in a few nags each time they were together.

She loved her maddening mother, and truly believed all the pushing and stage-mothering had been well-intended. Paula Healey loved her children—maybe a little too much—and wanted only the best for them, even if it meant stepping in to handle their affairs herself if she thought it necessary. She was the very definition of a "helicopter parent." Alexis tried to remind herself of those things whenever her mom drove her crazy. She supposed her exasperation was normal, considering. Their family had always been complicated, to say the least.

She locked her car door by habit after taking out the leather tote that held her computer tablet and other business items. The afternoon was cool but sunny, requiring no more than a light jacket over her thin sweater and slacks. The first green shoots of spring had appeared here and there in the gardens, and she spotted a few very early daffodils in the beds.

A bright yellow sports coupe drove into the parking lot and stopped in front of her. Paul Drennan, Bonnie's new husband, opened the driver's door, climbed out and leaned back against the car with his arms crossed over his chest, smiling down at her from his six-foot-four height. He looked more like a rangy cowboy than the high school math teacher she knew him to be. She would bet he was the subject of more than a few teen fantasies, she thought with a faint smile, remembering a harmless crush she'd once had on a high school history teacher. "Hello."

"Hi, Alexis." He glanced around the otherwise

empty parking lot. "Are you looking for Kinley and Bonnie?"

"I'm expecting clients to arrive shortly, and then we have a meeting with Kinley."

He nodded. "She's probably inside. Bonnie's at the hospital with her brother, but she should be back soon if you need to see her, too."

Alexis felt her diaphragm give a little jerk. "Hospital?"

"Yes. Zach, a college student who works part-time for Logan, had to have an emergency appendectomy today. He was working here this morning when he doubled over. Logan rushed him to the hospital in Zach's car, then stayed with him while contacting the kid's family. Bonnie went to pick up Logan and check on Zach, who's going to be fine, by the way. She called to let me know what was going on."

She busied herself for a moment by unnecessarily adjusting her glasses on her nose, speaking with what she thought was credibly casual concern. "That must have been scary for all of them. I'm glad Zach is going to be okay."

She didn't want to think too hard about her instinctive reaction at hearing that Logan was at the hospital. Something about the way Paul had worded the comment made her believe initially that Logan was the patient, and her mind had immediately filled with scenarios of accidents he could have suffered while working around the grounds. She reminded herself that she and Logan had only a casual relationship, so she had, perhaps, overreacted a bit—but then she reassured herself that it was only natural for her to be concerned for a friend's well-being. Everything was still comfortably under control. She didn't have to worry that she was letting herself care too much for Logan.

"Here are my clients now," she said as a dark sedan with a familiar driver pulled into the space next to her own.

Paul opened his car door again. "Kinley should be waiting inside. Have a good meeting."

"Thank you." She waved as he drove around the side of the building toward the downstairs apartment he now shared with Bonnie. Then she turned to greet Sharon Banfield and her newly engaged daughter, Liberty, who were here for a tour of the wedding facilities.

Kinley was her usual enthusiastic, briskly professional self, welcoming the Banfields and Alexis to the inn, giving a quick overview of the services offered to potential clients and their out-of-town guests, then taking them on a complete and informative tour of the inn and the grounds. She greeted the few guests they passed with a warmth that seemed quite genuine while showing Liberty and her mother all their inn's amenities without a high-pressure sales pitch.

After a walk through the gardens, where Kinley described the flowers that would be in bloom in early June of the following year, the date Liberty wanted to reserve for her wedding, she led them into the newly constructed ladies' dressing room and restroom beneath the wide back deck. Kinley's visible pride in the new facilities made Alexis smile, especially since she knew just how much work Logan had put into pleasing his sisters with those recent additions.

And speaking of Logan...

She looked around with everyone else when he came from the side of the inn, wearing his work clothes of jeans, boots, T-shirt and gray jacket, his dark hair looking disheveled. She had become an expert at hiding the punch of reaction she always felt when she saw him in front of other people, and she was confident no one knew that beneath the tailored jacket she wore with her spring-green sweater and charcoal slacks, her heart was beating a happy tap dance.

He nodded, not a hint of special interest on his face when he included Alexis in his greeting to the group. "Ladies."

Kinley introduced Logan to Liberty and her mother, then added with a wave toward Alexis, "And of course you already know Alexis."

"Yeah, sure. How's it going, Alexis?"

"Very well, thank you. I heard you had some excitement around here today."

"One of my crew took ill, had to be rushed to the hospital. He'll be okay, though."

"I'm happy to hear it."

"My brother is the one who supervises outdoor setup for the weddings," Kinley explained to their visitors. "He and his crew decorate the gazebo and gardens as requested, place the rows of folding chairs for guests, basically anything having to do with the outdoor part of events that isn't hired out to outside contractors."

Liberty smiled eagerly. "My friend Mandy had her wedding here last spring—she had the Tuscan theme? Very Italian, and it looked amazing."

Both Kinley and Logan nodded in recognition of the reference. "It was a pretty wedding," Kinley said to Alexis. "Mandy wanted lots of grape clusters and wine bottles and brick-red and olive-green buntings. She even managed to find a few oak wine casks for decoration. Logan set them in place where she wanted them and then we arranged groupings of candles and wine bottles on them with artificial grapes draped over the sides."

"Sounds lovely."

"It was," Sharon agreed drily. "Too bad the bride moved home to her mother two months later."

Liberty waved a hand dismissively. "Adjustment issues," she said lightly. "She and Blake are back together now. Mostly."

Alexis had to make an effort not to look at Logan. Because she didn't, she wondered if he was deliberately not looking at her, either. But still she sensed he shared her admittedly cynical reaction to the update.

"Anyway," Liberty continued, "I had an idea for my wedding theme…"

Logan made a low sound that Alexis interpreted as a swallowed groan. Kinley shot him a quick, stern look before saying encouragingly to the bride-to-be, "What's your idea, Liberty?"

"Well, my fiancé…" She giggled at the word, proving how new it still was to her, and flashed her ring in the late-afternoon sun. "My fiancé went to school in Baton Rouge, Louisiana, and now he's this huge New Orleans Saints fan. You know, football?"

Kinley nodded. Alexis swallowed, as this was the first she'd heard of a possible theme for the wedding she'd been hired only a couple days earlier to organize. Already she suspected what theme Liberty was considering, and she was proved right when the young woman blurted, "Mardi Gras! We can have beads and masks and lots of streamers and colored lights and balloons and stuff. Maybe some green and yellow and purple curtains hanging on the gazebo. And you know what would be really cool? Some of those big papier-mâché heads scattered around the gardens. Ooh, and maybe Steve and I could arrive on a Mardi Gras float that really moves, like pulled by a tractor or horses or something."

This time Alexis couldn't resist looking at Logan. He gazed back at her with a scowl that made it clear he expected her to rein in her client before she started asking for wrought-iron balconies and a steamboat.

Before Alexis could speak, Liberty's mother gave a laugh and patted her daughter's shoulder. "Take it down a notch there, sweetie. You're getting carried away."

Sharon shook her head indulgently as she looked at the others. "Liberty tends to go overboard when she lets her enthusiasm get away with her. She's just so bright and creative, it's hard to contain it sometimes."

"New Orleans and Mardi Gras are both very workable themes," Kinley told them gently. "I'm sure Alexis can help you come up with some beautiful and feasible ideas."

"Of course," Alexis assured them all. "I've organized Mardi Gras parties before. This would be my first Mardi Gras wedding, but we can definitely work with the theme."

"We'll have to think about this a bit more," Sharon said. "Just yesterday she was talking about a Japanese theme. We'll consult with her fiancé and come up with a final choice and then we'll call you for another appointment, Alexis."

"Yes, of course."

Sharon looked at her watch. "Now, if you'll excuse us, we really must be going. We're having dinner with her fiancé's parents this evening and we need to change. No need to walk us to our car. Thank you for the lovely tour, Kinley. It's going to be the perfect spot for my daughter's wedding, no matter what theme she chooses. Nice to meet you, Logan."

Mother and daughter hurried away, climbing the terraced steps to the side lawn and disappearing around the building. Liberty was still babbling about oversize decorations as her voice faded into the distance.

Logan barely waited until the pair was out of earshot. Hands on his hips beneath his jacket, he glared at both Kinley and Alexis. "Mardi Gras floats? Are you freaking kidding me? Or maybe she'll go back to her original Japanese idea and expect me to cut all the trees down to bonsai size and convert the gazebo into a pagoda. What the hell is wrong with just having a Blue Ridge Mountain theme, since that's where they're having their damn wedding?"

"Most of the weddings I organize are simple and elegant, highlighting the natural surroundings and simply using color combinations as theme," Alexis retorted coolly. What was wrong with her, anyway? Even as she was a bit annoyed by his attitude, she still found him incredibly appealing standing there all windblown and grouchy.

"Hmph." He turned his attention to Kinley. "And you. You just keep encouraging them, telling them we can pull off any cockamamy idea they come up with. I know you want to close the deals, but seriously, Kinley, you've got to cut back on some of these big-theme affairs before you bite off more than I can chew."

Kinley drew herself up stiffly, making an almost visible effort to speak in a professional tone when probably she would have liked to snap back at her brother, and very likely would have had Alexis not been standing there. She spoke pointedly to Alexis. "My brother doesn't mean we aren't interested in your future business, even for your more imaginative clients. We're happy to work with them as much as we can, aren't we, Logan?"

He merely grunted. Alexis bit her lip against a smile, avoiding his gaze.

"I have work to do," he said. "Alexis, nice to see you, as always."

"You, too, Logan," she replied politely. She made herself turn without watching him walk away, even though she loved watching him move in his sauntering, sexy way.

Kinley laughed ruefully and shook her head. "Sorry about that. My brother is in another one of his moods today."

"Yes, I noticed." And then, because that sounded perhaps as if she knew Logan a bit too well, she added quickly, "I have a brother, too. I recognize the signs."

"Older or younger?"

"Younger."

"Are you close?"

"No, not particularly," Alexis replied candidly.

Kinley didn't seem to know quite what to say to that, so she merely nodded. Alexis changed the subject to the couple who were considering the inn for their vows renewal ceremony. They would be arriving shortly to look around, and Alexis had no doubt Kinley would charm them with her usual skill.

She and Kinley talked mostly about business during their meetings, though they had strayed into somewhat more personal topics occasionally, usually when chatting about the history of Bride Mountain Inn. Through those casual conversations, Alexis knew a bit of Logan's family circumstances, but she didn't know how he felt about them. Facts, but no deep feelings, as suited a breezy affair. She and his sisters were on a very friendly basis, but she wouldn't call them her friends, exactly. Not the sharing-confidences-over-drinks or shopping-for-shoes-together type of friendship she had with Paloma, anyway. She thought they could be, but she was the one who'd maintained a slight distance between them.

She suspected Logan was the reason for her reticence. It was difficult enough carrying on a secret affair with him while working fairly often with his sisters; it would be much harder if she and Kinley and Bonnie spent even more time together away from their professional interactions. Not to mention that the more connected she became to his sisters, the stronger the ties between her and Logan became—and the more awkward it would be when it inevitably ended.

She and Logan had agreed that whatever happened between them, their work and their personal lives would remain entirely separate. On the job, they would be civil—his idea of civil, anyway—focused on optimal end results for both of them, even after they mutually agreed that the off-the-job affair had run its course. Completely rational and sensible.

Mentally crossing her fingers that the whole thing

wouldn't crash down around them despite their efforts not to become too emotionally attached, she forced herself to put Logan out of her mind and concentrate on her meeting with his sister.

Pebbles shifted beneath her snugly laced boot when Alexis placed her foot carefully into a depression on the steep hill rising in front of her on the following Tuesday. She adjusted her weight easily to find more stable footing. Pausing a few feet above her, Logan looked back over his shoulder, where he was carrying a small day-pack. "Okay?"

Settling the padded straps of her own pack a bit more comfortably on her shoulders, she grinned up at him. "All good."

He reached out a hand, and though she didn't really need the assistance, she placed hers in it, letting him haul her up beside him. His fingers tightened briefly around hers before he released her. "Need a water break?"

"Soon. It's a perfect day for a hike, isn't it?"

"Yeah, it's nice."

"Nice" was an understatement, in Alexis's opinion. The morning sky was a cloudless blue, the air crisp and fresh. A steady breeze tossed her low ponytail and kept them cool despite the exertion of the somewhat strenuous hike. Still winter-nude but showing the first buds of spring, deciduous trees towered around them, interspersed with fragrant evergreens. Through the bare branches, she caught glimpses of the stunning Catawba Valley view they would admire more fully from the apex of the well-worn path.

Five days after their last encounter at the inn, she

and Logan had driven separately to the hiking trail some forty minutes from Bride Mountain, meeting in the parking lot at the trailhead. They generally didn't go out together—this was the first time—but when she'd mentioned to him recently that she'd been thinking of taking a day off for a hike, he'd impulsively suggested this trek. He needed a few hours away himself, he'd added casually. He could be back at work by late afternoon to catch up on anything that required his attention. Because she had no appointments until six that evening, there was no reason for them to rush through this rare outing.

There was some risk, of course, that they'd run into someone who knew one or both of them, but the chance was slight. Though a popular destination, the trail wasn't crowded on this chilly weekday morning when most people were at work or school. In fact, they'd encountered only a handful of other hikers, none of whom they'd recognized.

When they'd first discussed taking the hike, Logan had pointed out that it wouldn't exactly be a tragedy if they did encounter someone they knew, though the chances were slim. There was no particular reason for secrecy about their friendship, other than the comfortable freedom from outside expectations. She wasn't quite as blasé about it as he'd sounded, uncomfortable with the thought of professional awkwardness if word got out they were seeing each other. Still, it was nice to be out together, to ignore everyone else and concentrate on each other and the lovely day.

They'd crossed several wooden bridges and passed a couple of primitive campsites in the almost four miles they'd hiked thus far. She stepped over a gnarled root that bisected the foot-flattened path, then glanced up at Logan again. Though the trail was rated as moderately strenuous, he handled it almost as easily as if they were walking on flat pavement. His slight limp proved no impediment to him, though it was somewhat more noticeable on the uneven ground. She wondered if it bothered him with this much exertion, but she knew better than to ask. His masculine ego would be dented at any suggestion he wasn't in peak condition—which, of course, he was, she thought, admiring the view of him from behind.

They paused beside a rushing stream still somewhat swollen from recent spring rains. Logan leaned against a tree trunk and drew a water bottle from his pack. He wore his usual jeans and T-shirt, though he'd switched out his work boots for sturdy hiking boots. He'd shed the windbreaker he'd worn earlier as he warmed from the exercise, stuffing the thin jacket into his pack.

Alexis found a relatively flat and reasonably clean boulder to use as a seat while she dug into her own pack. She wore lightweight gray hiking pants with a yellow scoop-neck T-shirt and a yellow-and-white windbreaker. She'd pushed up the sleeves of her windbreaker, but didn't remove it. The brisk breeze was a bit cool to her for short sleeves, though Logan seemed unaffected. She removed a square of microfiber cloth from her pack and cleaned her glasses, watching from beneath her lashes as Logan lifted his water bottle to his lips. Just seeing the way his strong throat worked with his swallows was enough to make her consider taking off her jacket, after all. Had the temperature just risen a few degrees, or was it simply her usual response to Logan's easy, innate sexiness that made her feel suddenly warmer?

She pushed her glasses back onto her nose, bringing him into even clearer, sharper view, then made herself look away long enough to dig out her own water bottle. Several long swallows helped her reinforce her temporarily shaky composure, though it wavered again when she lowered the bottle to find Logan studying her with an expression she well recognized—and which would have led straight to her bedroom had they been at her house.

He cleared his throat before speaking. "It's been a long time since I've made this hike. I used to come out here with Great-Uncle Leo when I was a kid. He was in his late sixties then, and could still run circles around me. I've heard it's usually crowded with tourists these days, but I figured it would be less so this morning."

She winked saucily at him. "I'm glad you were right. I rather like having you all to myself."

She took another sip of her water, then capped the bottle and stowed it again. Standing, she brushed a hand absently across the seat of her pants, though she wasn't particularly concerned about getting dirty on a hike. "Ready to forge on?"

"Almost." He pushed away from the tree in one fluid move, caught her in his arms and planted his mouth firmly on hers.

By the time the kiss ended, her arms were around his neck, their bodies were pressed full-length together and Alexis was definitely too warm for her jacket. She was grateful now for the breeze that ruffled her hair, brushed her cheeks and slipped inside her collar to cool her. She tipped back her head to peer up at him through her slightly askew glasses. "And that was because…?"

He chuckled as he released her with some reluctance. "Let's just call it an energy recharge."

She heaved a gusty sigh and glanced around. "Too bad we can't be entirely sure we're alone on the trail this morning."

He grinned and ran a hand down her back to give a light squeeze to her bottom. "Don't tempt me."

She so enjoyed flirting with him, seeing desire heat his hazel eyes to a gleaming gold. A ripple of arousal surged through her in response, and he must have seen it in her expression, because his fingers tightened for a moment before he made a show of stepping away from her. "Let's move," he said.

They'd made their way only a few yards farther before they came across a couple of overnight backpackers making their way back down the trail. She heard a low, wry chuckle from Logan before they exchanged polite greetings and a few casual remarks about the nice weather and the beautiful views.

The view at the top of the trail was well worth the effort of getting there. Beyond a stand of imposing stone monoliths, the path culminated at a rocky clearing that provided a breathtaking panoramic view for miles on this clear day. Jagged rock outcroppings jutted out over the sheer drop to the valley below, and a couple of daring college-aged boys posed recklessly on the edge for photos. Two young men who looked to be the same age hung back a bit, snapping pictures but staying well clear of the drop-off. A middle-aged couple hovered nearby, the man surveying the spreading vista through binoculars, the woman shaking her head in nervous disapproval of the younger hikers' antics.

Alexis had muted the ringer on her cell phone so it wouldn't disturb the peacefulness of the hike and had let the few calls she'd received go straight to voice mail to deal with later. Gretchen Holder, her administrative assistant, was handling calls at the office that morning and would text her if anything cropped up that Alexis had to handle personally. She couldn't resist lifting the camera-equipped phone to snap a couple of photos of Logan as he stood silhouetted against the deep blue sky, his profile turned to her.

As beautiful as the view was, she found her gaze turning to Logan more than to the distant mountains or the sprawling valley. Only when he pointed out a few landmarks did she force herself to focus on the scenery—Catawba Valley to the west, Tinker Cliffs to the north, the Roanoke Valley to the east. She imagined that the view would be stunning in the fall, with the brightly colored leaves spread like a patchwork quilt below, or in a few weeks in the spring when the mountain laurels bloomed, or in midsummer when all the shades of green draped the trees. Even now, with nature's colors still muted at the end of winter and just before the spring, the scene was stunning.

She raised the phone again, though she knew the camera lens could hardly begin to capture the beauty below. She heard a click and glanced around to realize that Logan had taken a photo of her in profile against the scenery. She smiled and he snapped again before lowering his phone.

"I wouldn't have pegged you as a phone photographer," she teased him.

He motioned vaguely to the camera-phones lifted around them. "Just trying to fit in."

She laughed softly, well aware that Logan couldn't care less if he "fit in." He was simply teasing her.

"Would you like me to take your picture together?" the woman Alexis had noted earlier asked a bit shyly from behind them.

Alexis and Logan shared a quick glance, then he shrugged. "Sure, why not?"

He draped his arm loosely around her shoulders after Alexis gave the woman her phone, and responded to the photographer's cheery command to "say cheese" with a silent smile. Photo taken, Alexis returned the favor and used the woman's phone to take a picture of the couple posed with the valley spreading behind them.

"You don't want to stand out on the edge of the point for a photo?" she teased when she returned the phone.

The woman rolled her eyes. "No, thank you! Those kids were scaring me half to death," she added, nodding toward the path down which the college boys had just disappeared.

A few minutes later, the other couple moved on, and Alexis was alone with Logan, though she doubted their solitude would last long. Relishing the soothing sounds of rustling breeze and calling birds, she drew a deep breath of the clean, fresh air as she watched a hawk circle lazily in the distance. "Beautiful," she murmured.

He reached out to tuck back a strand of hair that had escaped her ponytail, his fingertips lingering against her cheek. "Agreed."

Her pulse jumped, but she thought she managed to keep her expression serene as she said, "I needed this." She slipped her phone into her pocket. "A day out in nature, away from appointments and paperwork and unrealistic brides."

Logan shook his head. "How could they have this for inspiration—" he waved a hand toward the horizon "—and still decide to turn our grounds into faux Japan or Jamaica or Italy?"

She laughed softly and shook her head. "Maybe the ones who've grown up with this view tend to take it for granted. Though I grew up in Roanoke, I moved away straight out of high school for college in Maryland and then to New York City. I've only been back in the state for a year and a half, so it's all still fresh for me again. I'd almost forgotten how beautiful Virginia is."

She'd mentioned to him before that she'd lived in Maryland and New York, though they hadn't talked much about the years before they'd met.

"I grew up in the hills of Tennessee," he reminded her. "Beautiful countryside. Still, I don't take scenery like this for granted, no matter how often I see it."

No, she thought, he wouldn't. Logan was the type to appreciate what he had, without wasting time wishing it were something else. Wasn't that pretty much the way he seemed to feel about their no-strings affair?

He drew out his water bottle again and took a drink, then opened a zippered storage bag of trail mix and tossed a handful into his mouth. She shook her head with a smile when he offered the bag to her, but she pulled out her water bottle and sipped, taking advantage of the respite before the four-mile trek back down to the car.

She couldn't resist sitting on a ledge and dangling her feet over, though she chose a spot that looked a bit sturdier than the most outwardly jutting point. Logan sat cross-legged beside her, keeping his feet beneath him as he ate some more trail mix. "Sure you don't want some of this? I didn't take time for much break-fast this morning."

She smiled and held out her hand in surrender to temptation. He tipped a small pile of nuts and seeds into her palm and she munched as she swung her feet lazily below her. "That's a good mix. Do I taste a little cayenne pepper?"

He nodded. "Bonnie makes it for me. She knows I like things spicy."

He winked at her and a little laugh escaped her. Good grief, had Logan's sexy wink brought out her inner giggly schoolgirl?

"How hard are you going to have to work this af-ternoon to make up for taking the morning off?" she asked him after finishing her snack.

He chuckled. "I'll catch up. I left a list for Curtis to handle this morning. His retired brother-in-law is helping us out until Zach's cleared for work again after his appendectomy. How about you? Will you pay for taking a break?"

"I have a few calls to make this afternoon, and a six-o'clock meeting with clients, but other than that, it was a rare slow day for me. My calendar is packed full for the rest of the week, though."

"Big event this weekend?"

"Small shindig Saturday evening. Before that, on

Friday evening, I have to drive to Roanoke to endure another dinner party with my mother, my stepfather and her latest marriage prospect for me. I'm never sure whether he'll be a doctor, lawyer or candlestick maker, but I would place money on someone being there these days."

Logan frowned, slowly lowering his water bottle. "Marriage prospect?"

She reached up to straighten her ponytail, which had been loosened by exertion and the breeze. "My mother has been trying to marry me off for the past year, using every excuse from my advancing age to the fact that it isn't good for business for a wedding planner to be single. Let's just say, she's a rather... challenging woman," she added, choosing the word carefully.

"Your advancing age? Seriously? You're...what? Thirty?"

"Excuse me. I'm twenty-nine."

He nodded gravely. "Even younger, then."

"Mom was married—the first time—when she was twenty-two. Married my dad, her second husband, when she was twenty-five. She was forty-six when she married Duncan Healey, my stepdad, ten years ago."

"And your brother is twice divorced at twenty-seven," he grumbled, proving he'd retained what little she'd told him about her complicated family. "This is the path she thinks you should follow?"

She shrugged. "I guess she figures since I'm not going to be the musical theater star I grew up thinking I would be—and which she very much wanted me to be—I might as well provide her with a rich and successful son-in-law to brag about."

He raised an eyebrow. "The fact that you oper- ate your own successful business isn't brag-worthy enough?" he asked, without mentioning her reference to theater.

"My mom has owned and operated a successful floral shop in Roanoke for twenty-five years," she re- plied drily. "To her, being a business owner is no big deal. But she seems to be pleased that I've done so well with it so far. She takes credit for teaching me all I know about the business. And I suppose that's fair, though it wasn't what she'd always planned for me."

"I disagree. You've done an excellent job with your business, and I'm impressed with how much you've grown it since you bought it from Lula Coopersmith."

No compliment he could have given her would have pleased her more. She beamed at him. "Thank you, Logan."

Still frowning a bit, he nodded. "Just stating facts."

And then, as if concerned that they were straying a bit too closely to sentimental territory, he added brusquely, "As long as you're not trying to turn the inn into the Taj Mahal or Buckingham Palace, of course."

"You're starting on that again?" Trying not to grin, she shook her head. "Don't make me complain to Kin- ley that you're not fully cooperating with a client."

With one of his rare laughs, Logan stood and of- fered her a hand. "You're threatening to get me into trouble with my sister?"

Now she was the one to laugh as she allowed him to boost her to her feet, then slipped her arms around his waist. "I have much more effective weapons in my persuasion arsenal than threats," she said in her sultriest voice, pressing her body against his and looking up at him through her lashes.

She was rewarded with another flash of molten gold from his narrowed eyes just before his mouth covered hers.

She loved kissing him here in the sunshine with the wind whipping their hair, birds singing around them, the beautiful panorama spread below them. Loved having him all to herself, not worrying about who might see them together, feeling no need to keep her attraction to him under wraps. No pressure, no expectations, no questions or judgments, just two healthy single adults who enjoyed each other's company and shared an explosive chemistry.

Voices drifted up to them from the path, and they broke apart reluctantly. With a sigh of resignation, Alexis donned her day-pack just as a group of chattering middle-aged women came into view, some of them puffing a little from the climb. She and Logan exchanged cordial nods with them, then headed back down the path to retrace their steps to their vehicles.

The keys to his pickup truck in his hand, Logan stood close by until Alexis had unlocked and opened the driver's-side door of her car. "I'll give you a call later this week," he said.

She nodded. "It's going to be a crazy week from here out. I have no appointments at the inn this week, though I'll be there next week for final preparations for the Kempshall wedding next weekend. I'll be home around ten most evenings, if you want to call then."

"Yeah, I'll do that one night. So, I had a good time this morning."

She smiled up at him. "So did I."

"Have a great week. And, uh, good luck at your mom's matchup party?"

His dry, questioning tone made her smile wryly. "Good luck would be if I'm wrong about that. Maybe it'll just be family there this time."

She knew her expression wasn't overly optimistic. There'd been something in her mom's tone that had warned her to expect another maternal ambush. She would much rather spend that time relaxing with Logan, who expected nothing more from her than a good time. What more could she desire? she asked herself again as she made the solitary drive back to her rented house.

Chapter Three

"Maybe we could make it just a little bigger at this end?" Bonnie asked, critically studying her newly laid-out herb garden Friday evening. "Just to give me a little extra room for the rosemary plants."

It was too early in the season for planting, but Logan had the raised bed she'd requested ready for the first hint of warm weather. And already she was asking for changes? "I made it exactly to your specifications," he said irritably.

"I know, and it looks great," she assured him hastily. "But now that I see it finished, I just thought— Never mind, it's great. I love it, thank you."

And now he felt like a jerk for snarling at her. With a faint sigh, he reached out to squeeze her shoulder in apology. "Just let me know what adjustments you want. There's plenty of time to take care of it before it's warm enough to start planting. I'll put up fencing after you plant to keep the rabbits and deer out."

As was typical of his softhearted youngest sister, she moved closer to him and gazed up worriedly. "Are you not feeling well, Logan? You haven't been quite yourself today."

He forced a reassuring smile. "Just a little grumpy. Most folks would say I'm being totally myself."

Her answering smile was fleeting, her strikingly blue eyes still focused on his face with uncomfortable intensity. "Does your head hurt? You've worked so hard this week, maybe you need some rest."

"Bonnie, really. I'm fine. I'm sorry I snapped at you." He was uncomfortably aware that he didn't apologize easily, but Bonnie had a knack for making him feel guilty.

"Forget about the herb bed for now," she said briskly. "Come inside. I made a pot roast for dinner. All I have to do is warm the bread and we'll be ready to eat."

"I was going to spread some mulch in the east-side rose bed before calling it quits for the day."

"You can do that later. Come eat dinner. Rest awhile. I have cherry tarts for dessert," she added enticingly.

He groaned. "Okay, fine. I'll eat."

Bonnie laughed softly. "I figured the cherry tarts would get you."

"Oh, yeah."

His deliberately light tone seemed to set her mind somewhat more at ease, though he thought he still detected concern in her smile. He couldn't explain why he was so grouchy this evening. His mood had deteriorated steadily all day. Maybe his sister was right and he needed a break; he'd been working almost nonstop since returning from the Tuesday-morning hike with Alexis.

As expected, he hadn't seen Alexis since, though he'd spoken with her briefly on the phone last night. She'd been tired from a long day of meetings and paperwork and phone calls. He'd been perturbed by a long day of things going wrong—not to mention that it had been almost two weeks since he'd visited her bedroom. Those kisses on the hiking trail had been great, but decidedly frustrating.

In past months, their work had kept them apart for considerably longer than a couple of weeks, with only an occasional phone call to keep them in touch. Maybe he was getting a little spoiled because they'd had more time to spend together during the slower off-season. As the spring passed and bookings for both of them increased, they'd be lucky to get together once a month. For that matter, he never knew when they parted if they'd get together again, considering they had no commitment, no expectations. And he was good with that.

Hell, for all he knew, she could be meeting the perfect Dr. Right at her mother's house tonight, despite what she'd said about wishing her mom would stop trying to fix her up. Alexis had repeatedly implied that she wasn't interested in tying herself down to anyone in particular for now, at least until she'd spent a couple years making sure her business was solvent, but who knew? Maybe Dr. Right could change her mind.

Somewhat savagely, he dried his freshly washed hands on a towel in Bonnie's guest bath, then smoothed the scowl from his face and prepared to join his sister and brother-in-law for dinner.

"You should take a vacation, Logan," Bonnie suggested over cherry tarts a while later. "Before we get too busy with spring weddings. The grounds look great, and none of our upcoming events are so complex that Curtis and his brother-in-law can't handle them, especially since Butch Radnor is always available for temp jobs. When we shut down for those two weeks in January so Kinley and I could take off for our honeymoons, leaving you here to watch over the place by yourself, you promised you'd take some time off after we got back."

Those couple weeks here by himself hadn't been so bad, actually, though there'd been a snowstorm that had dumped quite a few inches on the grounds, requiring some quick action to prevent landscape damage. He and Ninja had been fine here on their own—and had been joined one night by Alexis. Taking advantage of having no family or guests at the inn to spot them together, she'd brought a bucket of chicken and a pan of homemade brownies and visited his bedroom for the first time, resulting in a few hours that still made him swallow hard when he mentally replayed them.

Mercifully unaware of the direction in which his thoughts had wandered, Bonnie continued, "If you don't take off within the next few weeks, we'll be well into the busy season and you won't be able to get away for more than a few hours at a time for at least another six or seven months."

Logan washed down a mouthful of tart glazed

cherries with a sip of the coffee she'd served with it. "I don't need a vacation."

He saw her exchange a look with her husband before she said, "You haven't had a vacation in at least three years, since we inherited the inn. Probably longer than that."

"I took off to go hiking just this past Tuesday morning," he reminded her, though he hadn't mentioned who his companion on the hike had been.

"And you were back by midafternoon," she retorted with a shake of her head. "That's not enough time off to really decompress."

"She's not going to give up, you know," Paul murmured over the rim of his coffee cup. "She's afraid you're headed for burnout."

"I'm fine. I take time off."

"You have gone out somewhat more during the past few months," she acknowledged. "But an evening out with friends every week or so does not count as a vacation."

She had no idea how much he enjoyed those evenings out with friends—especially since the friend in question was usually Alexis these days. It just seemed to have worked out that way. As a matter of fact, a couple more hours with her would go a long way toward the relaxation Bonnie was convinced he needed.

Though she was almost four years his junior, Bonnie had always been somewhat maternal in her manner toward him, especially since their mother died. The most domestic of the siblings, she loved cooking and decorating and taking care of others, which made her perfect for the general manager and chef role at Bride Mountain Inn. She'd been in the habit of fussing over him ever since a tumor in his left leg had struck him down in college, when she'd still been a senior in high school. He'd been pretty sick for a year through painful and debilitating treatments, but he had long since fully recovered. Bonnie knew that, intellectually, but there were still times when he suspected she looked at him and experienced painful memories, even though she knew he didn't want to talk about that time. As far as he was concerned, it was all in the past. No need to relive it.

His ordeal had left him more reserved than he'd been before, more prone to be somewhat of a loner—and a great deal more skeptical of promises and expressions of loyalty from anyone outside his family. He had absolute faith that his sisters would be there for him through thick and thin, whatever happened—just as he would be for them. Anyone else...well, he'd long since decided that having no expectations was the best way to prevent being disappointed or disillusioned again.

Because he *could* trust his sister implicitly—and maybe because she'd softened him up with pot roast and cherry tarts—he kept his tone indulgent when he said, "I'll let you know if I decide to take your advice. Now, I'd better head back to my place. Ninja's going to want his evening walk. Thanks for dinner, Bon. It was delicious, as always."

"Let me send a couple of tarts home with you for later."

He grinned. "I won't argue with that."

"It was nice to meet you, Alexis," Mark Fiorina said as he held her hand a bit too snugly in a good-night shake Friday evening. "I hope to see you again sometime?"

Turning the wish into a question made it clear he was fishing for her phone number, but she merely gave him a vague smile. "It was very nice to meet you, too, Mark," she said.

Though he'd seemed a little dense when it came to social skills during the evening, he must have picked up on her politely worded message that she wasn't interested in going out with him. Her mother's latest "prospect" was pleasant enough, if a little dull, but she had no desire at all to see him again. With a nod, he took his leave of her mother's home. Alexis intended to make her own escape almost immediately behind him.

"Honestly, Alexis, what was wrong with that one?" Paula Healey demanded from behind her daughter. Her hands were planted on her curvy hips, and her penciled brows creased beneath her salon-streaked ash-blond hair, making her bafflement clear. But then, that was the way her mother often looked at her. "He's a good man, a successful investment banker, and you didn't even give him your number, did you?"

"No, I did not. When are you going to stop these ridiculous attempts to fix me up with someone? I keep telling you, I'm not interested."

Predictably, her mom's lower lip quivered. "I just want you to be happy, Alexis. You need more in your life than work, you know."

"I *have* more in my life than work. I am perfectly happy. I need you to accept that and back off, Mother."

"I blame your father. Two nasty divorces set a terrible example for both you and your poor brother."

Alexis didn't even bother to point out that her mom had been involved in one of those nasty divorces, not to mention the years of acrimonious child custody fights that had followed. She knew her mother would argue that her current marriage was successful, though Alexis had always considered this one a rather calculated arrangement. Her mother, however, was the type of woman who needed to be married to feel secure, so whatever worked for her.

Alexis liked her stepdad just fine, though he was the reserved, brainy type who contributed little to a conversation unless it had to do with economics or American history. Like her mom, Duncan seemed content to be married for practical, socially advantageous purposes. They got along well, though they appeared to live almost separate lives from the same home, with different friends, different hobbies, different interests. Maybe they'd stay together, if for no other reason than because it would simply be too much trouble to split up. Maybe theirs was the best way to approach a marriage. No rosy-eyed illusions, no unrealistic expectations, no bitter disappointment when it didn't turn out to be everything they'd dreamed of in romantic fantasies.

Yet just the thought of getting into a long-term relationship with Mark Fiorina—or any of the other men her mother had paraded in front of her—made Alexis so depressed she just wanted to curl up in a corner somewhere. She would so much rather have fun with Logan for a short time than tie herself down for years to someone who didn't excite her at all. There was no way she was going to mention Logan to her mom, of course. Her mother would insist on know-

ing details and meeting him, interrogating them both,
which would ruin everything. Her time with Logan
was like a secret gift to herself, a private respite from
all the annoyances in her life.

Even now she could let her mind drift for a moment
to their kisses on the mountaintop and feel her irrita-
tion with her mom fading, letting her speak evenly.
"I really should be going. I've got an event tomorrow
and have to get an early start. I'll just go in and say
good-night to Duncan and Sean and the others before
I leave." Her brother had brought a date, and two couples who were friends of her mother's had attended
the dinner party, for a total of ten at the table. Perhaps
her mom had thought the number would make her fix-
up attempt less obvious. She'd been wrong, of course.

It was clear that her mom would have liked to
lecture awhile longer, but Alexis had become quite
skilled at evading those confrontations. Ten minutes
later she was in her car and headed home, to her relief. Despite everything, she loved her mom and her
brother and she was glad she lived close enough to
see them a couple times a month. But she was also
very glad that almost an hour's drive separated them
the rest of the time.

Logan and Alexis finally found a chance to get
together Sunday evening. He swept Alexis into his
arms almost the minute he closed her door behind
him. Though it had been only one day short of two
weeks since his last visit, he had barely enough patience to make it to her bedroom before stripping off
their clothes. He didn't actually pop buttons or rip
seams—he still maintained some self-control—but

he had to admit he was made perhaps a bit clumsier than usual by his impatience.

It was a nice boost to his ego that Alexis seemed as hungry for this as he was. He felt the tremors in her hands when she tugged at the hem of his shirt, heard the catch in her breath when they were finally skin to skin, felt the pounding of her heart when he covered one warm, taut-tipped breast with his hand. He loved the way she gasped and arched when he nipped his way down her stomach to her thigh, when he strung hot, wet kisses down the inside of her leg to her knee and back up again. Savored the choked sound she made when he placed his mouth on her.

With an arousing growl of frustration, she tugged at his shoulders, pushed at him until he lay on his back, straddled him with a reckless laugh that heated his blood close to the boiling point. And when neither of them could hold out any longer, they rolled on her soft white sheets, mouths and bodies fused, their pleasure expressed in low moans and incoherent murmurs.

They were in no hurry to leave her bed afterward. Propped on one elbow, Logan rested his head in his hand and gazed down at her as he smoothed a strand of hair from her damp face. "So, now that we've got that out of the way…"

She laughed at his paraphrase of her comment the last time he'd visited her bedroom. "I'm surprised we didn't break the bed."

He grinned briefly. "The night's not over yet."

She laughed again. "Sounds promising."

They were teasing, of course. He wouldn't spend the whole night with her. Another hour or so and he'd have to head back to the inn. Which was just as well.

He'd never been much for those stilted morning-after conversations.

She glanced toward the doorway. "I'm sure Fiona's still sulking in there because you didn't bring Ninja."

"Maybe an extra treat will help her get over it."

Smiling, she nodded. "Maybe."

"I'll give her an extra ear rub before I go."

She eyed his expression. "You're in a good mood this evening."

How could he not be, after such great lovemaking... such great sex, he corrected himself immediately. "Yeah, I guess. It was a long week, lots of annoyances. Feels good to get away from the inn again for a couple hours."

She frowned a little as she reached up to stroke his face in a soothing gesture. "You do look a little tired. Maybe you need a vacation."

He grimaced. "Now you sound like my sister."

"Which one?"

"Bonnie. She's been nagging me to take a vacation."

Alexis shifted onto her side, bunched her pillow beneath her cheek and studied his face. "Aren't you interested in getting away for a few days? You said yourself it feels good to leave the inn occasionally. Considering you basically live at your office, no one could blame you."

"Where would I go?" he asked with a shrug.

"Don't you have family you'd like to visit? Or someplace you've always wanted to see?"

"I see family every day," he said in amusement. "And I can't think of any place I'm dying to see at the moment."

"You could visit your dad," she suggested, suddenly sounding a bit tentative. "Have you ever been to New Zealand?"

He felt his eyebrows drawing down into a scowl and deliberately smoothed them. "Just saw my dad in December. That'll hold us for a year or so."

She backed off quickly from that topic, obviously sensing it led down a path he didn't want to take. "So, did you ever have a yen to visit the Pacific Northwest? Seattle, maybe?"

He was momentarily taken aback by that question. He happened to know Alexis would be in Seattle for a seminar the week after next. Surely she wasn't suggesting he accompany her?

"You know I'm going out for a seminar the last week of March," she said as if echoing his thoughts. "I just thought maybe you could fly out to join me for a couple days? The seminar is only a day and a half—Wednesday and part of Thursday—but I'd already decided to stay through the weekend, so I booked my room through Sunday."

She named the hotel, adding that it was on the waterfront, in a tourist-heavy part of town. "I'll have quite a bit of free time and I've never visited there before, and it would be fun to have someone to go sightseeing with, though I've heard this is hardly the optimum time of year to vacation there. Event planners have to schedule our conferences in off-season, and it was the West Coast's turn to host."

Out of all that babbled explanation, he focused on only one point. "You want us to go away together?"

She waved a hand dismissively, her tone studiously casual. "No need to make any announcements about

it, you know. It was so nice when we slipped off for
our hike the other day. I just thought it might be fun
to spend a couple days in a city where there's almost
zero chance anyone would recognize us and make a
big deal of it. You'd get a short vacation, I'd combine
work with play, then we'd return home and dive back
into our separate busy seasons. Considering my upcoming schedule and probably yours, too, we'll be
lucky to have a free evening to see each other until
winter."

He didn't like the sound of that. He really had gotten spoiled by seeing her fairly often, by both of them
having free evenings to spend together. With the busi-
est season of the year coming up for her, especially,
he had no doubt that would change soon. While his
workday started early and usually ended by the time
darkness fell, Alexis would have events or appointments nearly every evening, especially weekends.
She'd mentioned that she would be working several
out-of-town events in coming months, even after the
seminar.

She seemed to look forward to that impending
crazy, hectic time, which he supposed boded well for
her clients and her bottom line, but rather pushed him
to the sidelines. As it should be, of course. Her career
should definitely take priority over a loosely defined
affair, no matter how great the sex.

She smiled and shook her head. "It was just an impulsive suggestion. Maybe you can take a couple days
to go on a hike or mountain-bike ride, set up camp and
drink beer with a couple of your guy friends. That's
my brother's idea of a good time."

He'd never met her younger brother, nor any other

members of her family. "I've spent a few great weekends camping and drinking beer with pals myself.
Not a bad way to wind down."

"Bonnie told me she and Paul enjoy horseback
riding on their days off. Mountain trail rides at his
friend's stables. Sounds like fun. Kinley mentioned
that she and Dan like visiting museums and galleries
and sampling new restaurants for Dan to review in
the magazine he writes for."

"Kinley got that from our dad. He's what they call
a foodie. Every time he visited us when we were kids,
he took us out to restaurants that served foods we
didn't normally eat—and at least one annual trip to
Dollywood in Pigeon Forge, Tennessee. Dad has a
rather disturbing obsession with Dolly Parton," he
added drily.

"Hey, Dolly's a brilliant songwriter."

He groaned. "You have no idea how many lectures
I've heard on that subject."

"'Coat of Many Colors,' 'Jolene,' '9 to 5,' 'Hard
Candy Christmas'…"

With a low growl, he pulled the pillow from beneath his elbow and made a show of threatening to put
it over her face. She batted it away, laughing, and he
told her he had better ways of silencing her—which he
then proceeded to demonstrate, changing her laughter
to moans of pleasure.

It was late by the time he finally donned his jacket
and prepared to leave. He gave one last pat to Fiona,
who wound around his ankles once, then sat on a rug
to groom herself. Though he was probably just pro-
jecting emotions onto the cat, he couldn't help thinking she was still annoyed he hadn't brought her dog

buddy tonight. Alexis laughed when he suggested the possibility. "She'll get over it. And maybe next time you can bring Ninja."

He wasn't sure when that next time might be, considering everything, but at least she didn't seem to be annoyed that he'd patently avoided her suggestion that he join her in Seattle. Maybe it really had been just an impulsive idea, and she hadn't particularly cared one way or another if he accepted. She'd have a good time with him or without him.

"I'll think about what you said, okay?" he said gruffly. "The Seattle thing, I mean."

Her eyebrows rose, almost as if she'd already forgotten the conversation. "Yeah, sure. The invitation stands, if you're interested."

He kissed her good-night, then took his leave. He made the drive home with a frown knotting his eyebrows. The strength of his temptation to book an immediate flight to Seattle worried him a little. Okay, it sounded great to spend a few days in a new city with a beautiful, sexy companion. But what bothered him was that he suspected he wouldn't have been nearly as tempted if anyone other than Alexis had issued the invitation. And he was pretty sure he was going to miss her while she was gone.

Which meant, he decided, that he should definitely decline her offer. Maybe he'd been spending a little too much time with Alexis lately. He didn't want to get into the habit of expecting her to be there whenever he wanted her company. As he'd learned all too painfully in the past, depending on anyone other than his immediate family to always be there for him—even if, unlike Alexis, they promised to do so—all too often led to heartache. He'd had enough of that pain. He wasn't risking it again.

Most winter and early-spring weddings at Bride Mountain Inn were held indoors. The pretty front parlor, where his sisters had married, was perfect for smaller, more intimate affairs, and the big dining room, with its beautiful woodwork and antique chandelier and many windows to make the most of the views, served for larger events.

Afternoons could be cold and wet on Bride Mountain from December through mid-April, so brides who wanted to wed outdoors during that season took their chances with the weather, but still some chose to do so. Alexis had overseen a couple of Christmas-season outdoor weddings that had made the most of beautiful decorations and portable outdoor heaters. She'd even provided rented blankets for guests at one of the events, and the weather had cooperated by staying clear, though cold. Even during the nicest springs, summers and falls, it was necessary to have backup plans for unexpected bad weather. Still, it was always nerve-racking preparing for off-season outdoors events, as with the upcoming Kempshall wedding scheduled for Saturday afternoon.

Josie Kempshall had attended high school with Alexis, and had been one of the first to sign with her when Alexis took over Blue Ridge Celebrations. Josie had been newly engaged at the time, and it had taken several months for her and her fiancé to choose a date and venue, but she'd been adamant that she wanted Alexis on board no matter what the final plans would turn out to be. Despite Alexis's suggestions that she

might want to consider alternative ideas, Josie had ultimately set her heart on an outdoor afternoon wedding in March, the month in which she and her fiancé
had first met. Plan B was to hold the ceremony in the
dining room, and the guest list had been winnowed
accordingly, but the bride had made it clear that her
first choice was the garden, bare branches and all.
Alexis had obsessively monitored weather reports,
and was heartened to see that there was little chance
of precipitation that weekend, with the temperature
hovering in the mid-sixties for the afternoon.

"Let's hope the weather forecasters are right this
time," Kinley said during a final organizational meeting with Alexis and Bonnie prior to the event. Kinley
held up crossed fingers as she spoke. "So far, so good
for a nice weekend."

"If only the rain holds off until the start of next
week, as predicted, everything will work out fine,"
Alexis agreed.

Pragmatic Bonnie shrugged. "It wouldn't be the
first time we've frantically decorated the dining room
at the last minute, if necessary. Probably won't be the
last time if we have to do it this weekend. The wedding will be beautiful, no matter what."

Alexis nodded. At least the theme Josie had chosen for her wedding was fairly easy to coordinate.
She wanted the event to celebrate the start of spring,
using the colors of the daffodil as her inspiration—
the rich green of leaves and the crisp white, bold yellow and bright orange of petals and coronas reflected
in clothing and decorations. Redbuds, dogwoods and
silver bell trees were just coming into bloom on the
grounds and surrounding mountainside. Pots of daf-

fodils and white and yellow tulips would be gener-
ously arranged to make up for the sparse color in the
not-yet-in-bloom flower gardens. A few outdoor heaters would be strategically arranged near the rows of
folding seats—just in case.

In lieu of a sit-down meal, Josie had opted for hors
d'oeuvres and desserts at a reception on the grounds
following the ceremony. She didn't want a tent, but instead a casual arrangement of tables on the side lawn.
The reception theme was a spring picnic—more daffodils and tulips arranged in canning jars and metal
pitchers, gingham checks and polka dots on ribbons
and linens, a bluegrass band playing from a wooden
farm wagon as their stage.

Logan was not at all happy about the wagon. With
the grounds still soft from spring rains and the grass
still replenishing itself from snow cover, he worried
about wheel tracks and ruts in the meticulously leveled
side lawn. Though he hadn't spoken with the client,
he'd grumbled plenty to Alexis and Kinley. Kinley
had reminded him that since they'd reopened the inn
they'd hosted weddings with oversize tents, complete
with chandeliers and dance floors, an assortment of
charity functions including a couple of carnivals, two
Easter egg hunts, and a sweet sixteen party that had
included a rock band and more balloons than they'd
find at a traveling circus. The lawn had survived all
that, despite his complaints each time. Alexis noted
that Kinley carefully avoided mentioning the unfor-
tunate sandbox incident.

Though Logan wasn't appeased by the litany of
challenges his landscaping had endured, he stopped
fussing and went back to work while Bonnie excused

herself to head inside to see to their guests. Once again, Alexis was fairly confident Kinley and Bonnie had no clue that she and Logan had seen each other outside of their semi-regular work confrontations. Either Logan really was capable of switching his emotions on and off like a lightbulb, completely compartmentalizing his work and private lives, or he was an actor worthy of awards. She'd worked with performers on Broadway who hadn't been as convincing.

She had set her leather bag on the low rock retaining wall at the foot of the steps up to the side lawn while she and the Carmichael siblings discussed the reception. She turned to retrieve it, only to be startled to find it gone. Even as she wondered for a moment if she really had left it there, she caught a streak of black and brown out of the corner of her eye. She spun in that direction just as Kinley called out, "Ninja! Bring that back right this minute. *Logan!*"

The dog danced just out of arm's reach, holding the tote bag in his mouth, his amber-brown eyes seeming to twinkle with good-natured mischief. Shaking her head in amusement, Alexis knelt and held out one hand. "Bring me the bag, please, Ninja."

She would have almost sworn that the sound he made was a satisfied chuckle as he approached her and dropped the tote in front of her. Other than a little doggy spit, she saw no marks on it. "Thank you," she said, and he chuffed and wagged his tail.

"Silly dog." She rubbed his ears, then laughed softly when he crowded closer to her, nuzzling her face and making his goofy rumble-purr.

"Wow, he likes you," Kinley commented with a shake of her head.

"I've met him here before," Alexis replied lightly. "And dogs know an animal lover when they see one."

"Sorry." Logan stepped up to take a firm hold of his dog's collar. "He ran past me when I opened the back gate to my yard to get something out of the tool-shed. He doesn't usually do that."

He met Alexis's eyes briefly, and she got the un-spoken message that he thought Ninja had rushed out because he'd known she was there. She smiled and gave Ninja one last pat, though she was probably re-warding him for naughty behavior, then straightened and smoothed her clothes absently with one hand. "No problem. He was just being mischievous."

"That dog," Kinley said with a frown, "is the bane of my existence. I can't tell you how many times he's stolen something from me or Bonnie and hidden it under a rosebush or behind a bench or in Logan's yard. Oddly enough, he rarely steals from the guests, but our stuff is fair game to him. Taking your bag is somewhat out of character for him."

Alexis shrugged good-naturedly. "You were stand-ing here when he snatched my bag, so he was prob-ably toying with you."

Logan shook his head. "Now you sound like my sisters, ascribing human emotions to a dog. Kinley thinks he deliberately tries to drive her crazy, and Bonnie keeps talking about his 'quirky sense of humor.' He's a smart dog, sure, but I doubt his ac-tions are quite that calculated."

Looking at the broad grin on Ninja's broad, brown-and-black face, Alexis wasn't so sure, but she didn't bother to argue.

"Oh, what a beautiful dog!" Josie Kempshall hurried down the steps from the deck, followed more slowly by her fiancé, Ted Beecher. "He's part rottie, isn't he? I had a rottie when I was growing up, and I adored him."

Though Alexis suspected Logan was in a hurry to return Ninja to his yard and get back to work, he lingered long enough to let the bride-to-be fawn over the dog, who happily allowed himself to be hugged and admired. After a moment, Josie straightened and dusted off her hands. "Sorry, but I just love dogs," she said with a laugh and a toss of her long blond hair. "Especially rottweilers."

"Ninja is my brother's dog," Kinley explained. "He's not usually out without a leash, so he won't disrupt your wedding Saturday afternoon."

Josie grinned and waved a hand to indicate her lack of concern. "He'd be welcome, as far as I'm concerned."

Ted chuckled. "Josie's still hoping the ghost bride shows up as a guest. Having a dog crash the party wouldn't even make her blink."

Alexis saw Kinley's smile waver at the reference to the inn's resident legend. Logan made a sound that might have been a swallowed groan. The Carmichael siblings had never been enthused about exploiting the tale of the ghost bride for their business.

Alexis knew the tragic story, of course, as did most people from around these parts. It was said that long before an inn was built on this mountain, a young bride had died here the night before her wedding to her one true love, after overcoming many challenges to be with him. Ever since, she had haunted these grounds, revealing herself only occasionally—and only to couples who were destined to love each other until death. Bonnie had confided to Alexis once that her great-uncle Leo and his dear Helen had seen the bride on the night they became engaged. Logan and Kinley had never believed the story, but she always had, she'd added with a misty smile.

Logan didn't like talking about the ghost. He'd told Alexis once that the whole thing was just a sentimental old story no rational person could possibly believe, but he tried to be polite when guests of the inn referred to the legend. She knew how difficult that must be for him, when she was sure he'd rather have scoffed openly.

"If you'll excuse me," he said, "I need to take the dog to my place, then get back to work."

Alexis told herself it was okay to watch him walk away because the others were, too. But maybe they were paying a little more attention to the dog gamboling happily at his side than to the sexy way Logan moved.

She made herself turn away to focus on the meeting with her clients, considering their last-minute requests, assuring them that all the vendors had been contacted and were ready to go and that all their wishes for the wedding would be fulfilled to the best of her ability, a sentiment echoed by Kinley on behalf of the inn. She gave her entire attention to her work during that discussion, pushing thoughts of Logan to the back of her mind. There would be plenty of time to think about him later when she was at home alone with her cat.

She was tired and hungry by the time she set a plate of stir-fried vegetables and rice on her table that eve-

ning. Sinking into her chair, she sprinkled soy sauce
over her dinner, picked up the chopsticks she was
using just for fun, then glanced at the cat, who sat on
the floor beside her, cleaning her face after finishing
her own dinner.

"By the way, I think Ninja sent his regards," she
said, breaking the silence in the room.

Fiona glanced up at her a moment, her pointed ears
cocked, then went back to her grooming.

Alexis took a bite of her food, her thoughts wandering as she chewed. She thought about her schedule for
the next day, about the Saturday afternoon wedding,
about the list of things she had to see to beforehand.
She thought of a message she'd received from Paloma
earlier, about a new boy toy in Paloma's life, and she
promised herself she'd call after dinner to catch up
with her friend.

Funny, the longer she spent here in Virginia in her
new career, it became harder to remember the life
she'd pursued before. Living in her tiny studio, shuf-
fling through city crowds, attending endless classes,
auditions and parties, working part-time florist jobs to
pay the bills. There'd been a man—one who'd dazzled
her and entertained her and promised to love her forever. Despite her disillusioning experiences with such
promises in her own family, she'd almost let herself
believe him. She'd hoped he cared enough about her to
support her in whatever goals she pursued, but when
she'd told him she was giving up performing to open
her own business, he'd dumped her like a hot potato.
It turned out that Harry had been more enamored of
her profession, and of the exciting acquaintances and

activities that had accompanied it, than he'd been with the real Alexis.

Maybe she'd have stayed in New York had things worked out with Harry, though it would have been more of a challenge to start a successful enterprise there with so much formidable competition. Instead, she'd bought the established company here, telling herself it would be easier to begin an all-new life by putting her old one completely behind her. And she'd been right. The business was going well, she was making new friends, though she'd put in so many hours at work that her social life had most definitely suffered, and she was confident that she'd made the best decision.

After the initial pain and disappointment had faded, she'd realized she hadn't been irreparably heartbroken by the end of her relationship with Harry, but it had only reinforced her skepticism about the validity of most cases of so-called romantic love. Give her honesty and clear-eyed realism any day over the deceptive throes of rose-tinted infatuation!

And speaking of bluntly honest realists...

She glanced at the phone that lay beside her dinner plate, wondering if Logan might call tonight. Probably not, since she'd seen him earlier that day. She wasn't sitting by the phone waiting to hear from him. She had quite a lot of paperwork to handle that evening, and she'd scheduled the next three hours or so to take care of that—after a lengthy chat with Paloma, of course.

Perhaps it was just as well that Logan hadn't jumped to accept her offer to join her in Seattle. Though as far as she knew they had no mutual acquaintances who would attend the seminar, and it was unlikely anyone would see them together and report back to their families, still it would probably change the dynamics of their easy, nebulous relationship to spend several days—and entire nights—together that way. They'd never even woken up together, she thought, toying with the remainder of her food.

Maybe all in all, it was better not to take the chance that she would like that just a bit too much. Remembering the debacle with Harry had reminded her of all the reasons she was being so careful not to fall for Logan, a man whose own emotional barriers were glaringly evident. She wanted to believe she was too wise these days to simply open herself up to potential heartbreak.

She had just turned off her computer and dressed for bed when her phone rang. Though she'd convinced herself he wouldn't call, she knew it was Logan even before she glanced at the screen. "Hello?"

"Hey. I hope Ninja didn't mess up your bag earlier. Because if he did, I'll—"

"No, it's fine. Just had to wipe off a little doggy drool. He was very careful with it. He was just playing with me."

"Yeah, I was hoping Kinley wouldn't pick up on how comfortable he is with you."

She forced a smile, though he couldn't see it. "Right, we wouldn't want that. But it was okay. She accepted that he was just fooling around."

"So, how did the rest of your day go?"

Her smile felt a bit more natural when she leaned against the headboard and pulled her knees up in front of her. "I do have a funny story for you. Someone told me about a wedding last weekend that had a dog for a ring bearer. So, anyway, right in the middle of the ceremony, the dog freaked out…"

They chatted pleasantly for some fifteen minutes before saying good-night. It was nice having the echo of Logan's deep voice in her mind as she snuggled into her pillow a few minutes later with her cat curled beside her. But even as she nestled into the pillows and pulled her blanket to her chin, she was aware that once again he'd carefully avoided any mention of her upcoming trip to Seattle.

Chapter Four

Alexis sat in her office Friday after lunch, a half-read contract displayed on her computer monitor, and several letters to be signed piled on her desk beside a stack of memos to be read and acted upon. It wasn't a large office, but she'd made the most of the space with open-backed, floor-to-ceiling white bookcases over peach walls, a glossy white desk and credenza set, and white leather seating. On the wall behind her desk were large framed photos of some of the weddings and other events she'd coordinated during the past year and a half.

There wasn't much of a view from the big window opposite her desk, merely a parking lot ringed by bare trees and flower beds that needed a bit of spring care, but the sun streamed in through the open blinds, adding even more light and airiness to the room. She'd never cared to work in dark offices, preferring the same bright whites and clear colors she'd used at home.

Someone tapped on her open office door and she glanced up from the monitor, absently pushing her glasses up on her nose. She smiled when she recognized her visitor. "Kinley. Hello, come in."

"Gretchen told me to come on back, but if this is a bad time…"

"Not at all." Alexis rose and motioned toward the comfortable seating at the other end of the office, a white leather couch and two matching wingback chairs grouped around a glass table that held a bouquet of fresh spring flowers and a couple of albums of wedding and event photos. "Please, have a seat. Would you like some coffee? Or tea? It would only take a couple of minutes to make either."

"Tea sounds nice, if you have time to have a cup with me. I just dropped off some new brochures for the inn with Gretchen and I wanted to say hello to you while I'm here."

Alexis moved toward the pod brewer on her credenza. "I'm glad you did. I always appreciate a pleasant distraction from dull paperwork."

"I know that feeling," Kinley said with a laugh, sinking onto the couch. "It seems like I can never catch up with the paperwork from either of my jobs, especially when I have a big real estate deal under way."

Alexis set a cup and saucer in front of her visitor and settled into one of the chairs with her own cup. "Josie called this morning. She's so excited that her wedding is finally going to happen tomorrow. She and Ted have waited a long time to see this day."

Kinley smiled. "She's great to work with, isn't she? So easygoing. I have a feeling her wedding is going to be so much fun for her guests."

"That's what she wants. A party on the grounds. Nothing formal or stuffy or overly traditional, which was why she didn't want an official rehearsal today. Nor did she want to put a whole lot of effort into it," she added with a wry smile. "That's why she hired me. She pretty much told me what sort of wedding she wanted, what colors she likes, and then just set me loose. Some of the details tomorrow are going to be surprises even to her."

"There's a world of difference between micromanaging brides and the ones who expect you to do everything for them, isn't there?"

Alexis laughed. "Definitely. But at least I know Josie isn't the type who'd put it all on me to decide, then criticize my choices."

Kinley nodded in empathy. "Been there."

"How's everything at the inn?"

Wrinkling her nose, Kinley picked up her teacup. "I think I'm going to make a new policy. Starting immediately, my brother will no longer be included in any meetings with clients or potential clients. Bonnie and I will make all future arrangements, then simply tell him afterward what we want him to do. We should have done that from the beginning. It's what he's always wanted, just to do his job, close himself back in his house and let us deal with guests and clients."

"What has he done now?"

Biting her lip, Kinley looked as though she wasn't

sure how much she should share with Alexis, who certainly fell more under the classification of "client" than "friend." But perhaps that delineation was fading a bit as they spent more time together, Alexis conceded, thinking of how much she liked both Carmichael sisters, how well they'd all gotten along from the start of their collaboration.

Kinley seemed to reach the same conclusion. With a crooked smile, she said, "I suppose you've worked with us enough to realize that customer relations isn't my brother's strong suit. Honestly, he's a great guy. The best brother anyone could ask for. He just— Well, he doesn't have much of a filter between his thoughts and his words when it comes to ideas he thinks are unrealistic."

Alexis laughed softly. "You don't have to defend him to me. I've never really minded his grumbling."

She thought it was safe to admit that much, at least, considering that she had worked so closely with all three of the siblings during the half dozen events she'd coordinated thus far at the inn. "He's done an excellent job for me each time, despite his, um, hesitation on certain issues. I can't really blame him for wanting to protect the grounds. He and his crew work so hard to keep them immaculate, and I'm sure he's always trying to protect them for future use. Some of your events are so close together that I'm amazed he can take down from one and set up for the next so quickly."

"Exactly." Kinley looked both pleased and relieved that Alexis understood. "You've always had a knack for handling him. Unfortunately, others don't understand him quite as well."

Alexis grimaced. "Something happened?"

"He had words with another wedding planner this morning, one who's coordinated several weddings at the inn. Or should I say, he didn't bother to mince words with her, and she didn't take it well. I think I managed to calm her down, and she said she wasn't taking us off her venue list, but she was really annoyed."

Alexis was a little surprised. Sure, Logan growled a bit, but she had never seen him be completely unreasonable. He'd even held on to his patience—for the most part—with an overanxious mother of the bride at one of her earlier weddings at the inn who wanted to stand over his shoulder and supervise his every move, until Alexis had sent her off on several "important" errands to keep her busy elsewhere. "Were her requests completely out of line?"

Kinley chose her words carefully, obviously aware that she was talking about another client. "She asked if it would be possible for us to cut down or at least severely prune back the big magnolia tree on the east side of the gazebo. She said a couple of her photographers have complained that it hampers full access to the ceremonies. I know it's tricky taking photos from that angle, but it's not impossible, and most of them come up with beautiful shots from all around the gazebo."

"Cut down that beautiful magnolia? That would be a crime!"

"That's pretty much what Logan said. Only maybe not quite so elegantly," Kinley agreed wryly.

"I won't ask the name of the other planner, because

I don't believe in gossiping about my competitors, but I will say I think that request was out of line."

"To give her credit, she wasn't pushy or insistent with the request, though she got defensive when Logan snapped at her. She said it was merely a suggestion. I would have turned her down more tactfully. Logan just didn't react well."

"I wouldn't think so." Alexis couldn't help biting her lip against a rueful smile when she pictured Logan's reaction to someone suggesting he cut down one of his carefully tended trees.

"Hence, my new policy. No more client meetings for Logan. I'm the liaison."

"That's probably a good plan. Though I don't mind if he wants to join in on our meetings in the future. I'm used to him by now," she added casually.

Kinley laughed. "You've always been able to handle him better than most outside the family."

"As I mentioned, I have a brother myself," Alexis replied lightly.

Kinley changed the subject then, to Alexis's relief. They chatted a bit about the preparations for Josie's wedding and then Kinley glanced at her watch and grimaced. "Guess I should be going. We both have a lot to do before tomorrow's wedding."

Alexis looked toward her desk and sighed. "I'm afraid so. But I'm glad you stopped by. I enjoyed the break."

Kinley stood and smoothed her tailored slacks with her left hand, on which gleamed a gold wedding set with a sparkling stone. "So did I. Thanks for the tea."

She paused in the doorway on her way out. "Alexis, just curious—are you seeing anyone?"

After only a momentary pause, Alexis replied candidly. "I'm seeing someone occasionally. Why?"

Kinley laughed rather sheepishly. "I had a sudden matchmaking inspiration. But never mind, it was probably a bad idea, anyway. I'll see you tomorrow."

Clearing away the remains of their tea break, Alexis thought of that odd exchange. Since they'd talked about Logan at the start of their visit, it was likely that Kinley had momentarily considered nudging her and Logan together. Ironic, but likely. And this, she thought somewhat wistfully, was why she hadn't made a stronger attempt to become close friends with Kinley and Bonnie. Too many potentially uncomfortable moments.

Maybe after she and Logan stopped seeing each other, she'd make more of an effort with his sisters. Invite them to dinner or something. Because she and Logan had made a pact from the start that the end of their affair would be amicable, uncomplicated, with no regrets and no repercussions on their future work collaborations, it shouldn't be awkward for her to hang out more with his sisters afterward.

Still, as much as she liked Kinley and Bonnie, she found herself hoping that change in their relationship wouldn't happen too quickly. She was enjoying those stolen hours with Logan too much to give them up just yet.

Any wedding without a rehearsal required a bit more effort on Alexis's part on the day of the wedding. Fortunately, the entire party had agreed to gather ninety minutes before the two-o'clock event, giving them plenty of time to run through the sequence of events, familiarize themselves with the setting and dress for the ceremony. Josie and Ted had no compunctions about seeing each other prior to the wedding—after all, they'd been living together for more than a year, Josie said cheerfully—so they mingled among their guests during the brief instruction session Alexis conducted. Bonnie had set out drinks and snacks on the deck, and the plates emptied rapidly.

"Where's that cute dog?" Josie asked at one point, looking around. "And his cute owner," she added with a wink. "I wanted to tell Logan what a great job he's done with the decorations."

Alexis couldn't argue with that. Logan and his crew had made the grounds look beautiful for the wedding. The big baskets of bright flowers had worked exactly as she'd hoped to hurry spring to the gardens. He'd draped garlands of ivy and daffodils around the gazebo, matching the clusters attached to the end of each row of folding white chairs. Cheery yellow, orange, green and white paper lanterns hung from tree limbs and danced in the light breeze, compensating for the leaves that had not yet unfurled. The result was a cross between an outdoor wedding and a casual garden party, exactly what Josie had requested.

She glanced toward the side lawn, where the post-ceremony celebration would be held. There, in lieu of a tent, Logan and his crew had erected tall metal poles strung across with wires. More paper lanterns hung from the wires, providing overhead color for the party. Long tables with yellow-and-white gingham linens sat ready to hold the picnic-style snacks to be served by the caterer Alexis had hired, and the rustic wooden farm wagon she'd rented had been pushed carefully into place at one end of the lawn. Decorated with baskets of bright yellow daffodils and white tulips, it would make a charming stage for the bluegrass band waiting to entertain the guests.

"Logan keeps his dog fenced in his backyard when he doesn't have him out on a leash. And if you don't get a chance to see him today, I'll be sure and pass along your compliments."

Josie smiled and gave Alexis an impulsive embrace. "You've done an amazing job, too. This is exactly the way Ted and I wanted to celebrate our wedding. Thank you so much."

Alexis laughed and returned the hug. "The wedding hasn't even started yet. I just hope nothing goes wrong."

Her friend and client waved a hand dismissively. "As long as everyone has a good time and Ted and I leave here legally married, I'll be happy. And I'm so glad you agreed to sing for us at the reception. I used to love to hear you sing in all those high school performances."

Thinking of all the years of training, practice and performances since those high school programs, Alexis smiled somewhat wryly. Performing at weddings was not something she wanted to make a habit of, but because Josie was an old friend and had been such an enthusiastic client, she'd agreed to do a number at the reception party.

"Oh, and there's one other thing."

Something about Josie's engaging smile and innocently widened eyes put Alexis instantly on alert. "What?"

"Ted has a really cute friend. Single. Makes good money. A great guy, and not bad-looking, either."

"Josie—"

"Anyway," the bride hurried on, "he's coming to the wedding, and I told him all about you. He's really looking forward to meeting you."

"Josie, really. I'm going to be very busy during the wedding and the reception. You've entrusted me to make sure everything behind the scenes goes smoothly, which involves a lot of supervision and co-ordination. I'll be too busy to spend much time with any one guest—even if I were interested in a fix-up. Which I'm not, by the way," she added firmly, wondering why everyone suddenly seemed so determined to match her up with someone.

Josie winked impishly. "Well, I'm going to introduce you, anyway. Who knows, it could be love at first sight."

Alexis didn't even believe in love at first sight, though as a wedding planner it was probably best that she not mention her romantic cynicism. "I'll be much too busy for that today," she said instead, with an airy laugh. "And speaking of which, you should be getting ready while I take care of a few last-minute details."

"Okay, I'm going." Josie waved to her mother and bridesmaids, who were also urging her to start getting ready. Never the type to hurry when ambling was so much more fun, she headed toward the dressing room, though Alexis noted she stopped several times along the way to exchange hugs and greetings with arriving friends.

With a little sigh, Alexis pulled out her tablet computer to go over her checklist one last time before the start of the wedding. She hoped Josie would be too distracted by the festivities to go through with her matchmaking threat.

She found herself glancing in the direction of Logan's cottage, realized what she was doing, then sternly turned her attention back to her responsibilities.

Logan generally stayed out of sight during a wedding or other event, emerging again afterward to start cleaning up. Usually he and Ninja sat in his living room with a seasonal sporting event on the TV while he worked on his computer. Kinley had asked him to make a few upgrades to the inn's website, and he had another project looming for his part-time consulting work. Today, however, he found himself unable to concentrate fully on software. Even Ninja paced the floor, looking out the windows and sighing occasionally.

Finally conceding to their mutual restlessness, he snapped a sturdy leash on Ninja's collar. "Let's go for a walk," he said, reaching for his jacket. "But behave yourself."

The dog grinned up at him with a deceptively innocent expression.

Surrounded by woods, with a creek rushing just beyond the roomy fenced yard, Logan's two-bedroom cottage was downhill on the east side of the inn. His one-car garage was accessed by a narrow private drive leading off the main road. A rough path through the woods connected with the six-mile hiking trail that started at the back of the inn's grounds. Weather permitting, Logan and Ninja walked that trail nearly every day, usually early mornings before he started working around the grounds.

Though he tended to be an early riser and woke ready to get going, he tried to make himself and his crew wait until nine to tackle any noisy projects out of consideration for later-sleeping inn guests. He hadn't had time for a long walk this morning, so he figured they might as well stretch their legs now while the wedding and reception were under way.

Pleased to be outside with him, Ninja trotted beside him, sniffing the air and ground, policing this land he considered his own. The black-and-brown dog had shown up on Logan's doorstep one winter morning more than a year ago, cold, wet and hungry. He'd been little more than an overgrown pup then, maybe a year old, a few pounds shy of the large size he'd attained since. There hadn't been a collar or an ID chip, but Logan had dutifully searched for an owner, anyway. By the time he'd concluded that no one seemed to be looking for the stray, Logan had bonded with the mutt.

He hadn't even known he wanted a dog at the time, probably would have declined if anyone had tried to give him one, but now he couldn't imagine making these walks alone again. "Quirky sense of humor" and all, Ninja belonged with him. The dog made it clear he felt the same way, seemingly content to stay in the fenced yard—most of the time—while Logan worked, and happily by his side before and afterward.

From a clearing at a high point on the path from his house to the main hiking trail, Logan could see the grounds of the inn spread below him, especially this time of year before the trees completely filled with leaves. He liked to pause here on his walks to survey his property—well, a third his, anyway.

He'd always known he and his sisters would inherit this place someday. Their mother's uncle Leo had told them so from the time they were just kids, since they were the only heirs to the Finley family legacy. Logan and his sisters had spent nearly every holiday and most summers here at the inn growing up, especially after his mom's parents in Tennessee died, and Uncle Leo had always put them to work around the place—not that they had minded, since he'd always made it fun.

Still, Logan had never thought he'd end up as care-taker here. He'd trained in computer sciences, started his own business—with a partner he'd trusted im-plicitly at the time—and figured that when the inn eventually became his, he'd either sell his third to his sisters or remain a silent partner. There had never been any question that Bonnie would run the inn someday. It had been her goal since childhood, and something she'd worked and trained for since. Kinley was a natural-born saleswoman, a trait that had served her well in the real estate business and now came in handy as she hustled business for the inn.

As for himself, he had a talent for computers, was good with his hands and had always been mechani-cally minded. Bonnie teased him about being a "Re-naissance man." With his previous business ending painfully not long before Uncle Leo died, he'd thrown all his skills and talents into renovations and mainte-nance, surprisingly finding refuge in his cottage and solace in the hard work and challenges of the inn. He had his family, his dog, his health, his truck. All in all, he was a lucky man. Wouldn't change a thing.

Standing there high among the shadows, he hadn't realized he was searching for Alexis among the milling crowd below until he spotted her. Dressed in her favorite bold red, with her dark hair gleaming in the afternoon sun, she stood out from the pastel-clad wedding guests—at least to his eyes.

The wedding ceremony had ended, and everyone had moved to the side lawn for the reception. The guests mingled around the food tables, sat in the folding chairs that had been carried up from the wedding rows, gathered around the happy bride and groom. A few hovered close to the area heaters, though Logan found the cool temperature comfortable enough in his jacket. The cheery bluegrass music being played by the quartet on the farm-wagon stage drifted up to where he stood, making his boot tap in time. This was the kind of wedding he could endorse. Low-key, comfortable, not overly decorated, but making good use of the beautiful setting provided by nature and Bride Mountain Inn.

He spotted Kinley working the crowd and Bonnie bustling near the food tables, but his attention turned almost immediately back to Alexis. She looked really good. Maybe before the weekend was over, he could tell her so. And he hoped his hands were on her when he did.

Ninja whined a little and moved toward the party, causing Logan to tighten his grip on the leash. "We'll see her later," he promised, as much to himself as the dog.

He was just about to turn away and continue his walk when something made him stop. He watched with a scowl as the bride—Alexis's old school friend

Josie—all but dragged a tall, somewhat lanky man over to Alexis and waved her expressive hands as if to indicate introductions. Even from this distance, it seemed obvious to Logan that an attempted fix-up was under way. Josie was doing everything but linking their hands together. He was grimly pleased when Alexis moved away only a few short minutes later. She walked toward the makeshift stage and he lingered to see if she was going to make some sort of announcement. He could just hear her voice from where he stood.

"Josie and Ted have asked me to perform one of their favorite songs as we celebrate their marriage today," she announced. "It's from Josie's favorite animated movie and Broadway show, *The Lion King.*"

Alexis had mentioned a couple of times that she'd studied music. That she'd performed occasionally since college, though she'd always been deliberately vague about when or where. He knew she'd lived in New York. She'd told him she supported herself primarily by working for florists, where she'd added to her experience in wedding planning begun in her mother's flower shop. Now, listening to her sing, he suspected she had deliberately downplayed the role music had played in her life before he'd met her.

She was good. Damn it, she was better than good, he thought with a hard swallow. She was amazing. Her clear, beautifully modulated voice wafted on the air to where he stood, and he could feel the power of it rippling through him. He stood transfixed, Ninja very still at his side, until the last note faded. The guests on the lawn applauded loudly, almost mobbing Alexis when she turned the program back over to the bluegrass band and stepped down from the wagon-stage, hiding her almost entirely from his view. He saw the tall, lanky man slip into the throng and make his way toward the center and the crowd parted just enough for Logan to see him reach Alexis's side, place a hand on her shoulder and smile down at her.

He turned away. He thought he saw a flash of white in the underbrush to his right, but when he looked that way, nothing was there. Either he'd imagined it, or it had been a bird or squirrel or deer. Quite a few types of wildlife made Bride Mountain their home, and Logan had never minded sharing, despite Bonnie's fussing about the critters getting into her garden.

He had to give a slight tug on Ninja's leash to get him moving in a direction opposite where Alexis was. For some reason, neither of them was quite as enthusiastic about the walk as they had been when they'd started.

An hour after the official end of the wedding reception, much of the cleanup had been completed. All the guests had departed except for the few who would be spending the night in the inn, all of whom had gone inside now that the event had ended. Alexis made sure all her vendors had done their part in the clearing away. Logan and two of his crew had already taken down most of the decorations. The bride's family had lingered after the newlyweds made their dramatic departure in a gaily bedecked convertible to load up all the gifts and the decor items Josie wanted to keep. The last carload had just been driven off.

Alexis was almost ready to leave herself. She

looked around to make sure there was nothing left for her to do.

Kinley approached her with a big smile. "Everything went very well, didn't it? I've heard nothing but compliments from the guests I've spoken with."

"It was a great wedding," Alexis agreed. "There were a few minor glitches, but that's to be expected, and the guests weren't even aware of most of them. Josie thought it was hysterically funny when the flower girl tried to take off her dress during the ceremony because it 'itched her neck.'"

"Are you kidding?" Kinley laughed. "Everyone thought that was adorable, except for maybe the flower girl's mother."

"Okay, the wagon's hooked to the truck and on its way back to the farm where it belongs," Logan reported, approaching them with what Alexis thought of as his stern "work face." "Everything else should be cleared away in another hour or so."

She bit her lip against a smile. She'd watched Logan fret about the placement of the wagon prior to the wedding and then supervise its removal afterward. He and his guys had carefully pushed the wagon by hand, as he'd refused to allow a truck or tractor on his grounds. Despite his complaints, he'd set it up beautifully, meticulously arranging the flowers and garlands to decorate it, and there had been many rave reviews from admiring guests.

"The grounds looked absolutely beautiful today," she said, including both Logan and Kinley in the warm praise. "This continues to be one of my favorite wedding venues."

Kinley, of course, preened a little. Logan nodded in acknowledgment of the compliment.

"Oh, and by the way," Kinley said, reaching out to touch Alexis's arm, "I was blown away by the song you performed at the reception. I had no idea you could sing like that! Logan, you should have heard her. Her voice is beautiful."

"Actually, I did hear her."

Alexis was startled, and Kinley looked surprised, as well. "Where were you? I didn't see you at the reception."

He shook his head. "Ninja and I were taking a walk," he explained, motioning toward the wooded rise beyond the gardens. "We could hear from the trail. You sounded good, Alexis."

She had no problem singing before an audience. She'd been doing so since she was just a kid. She hadn't been at all nervous climbing onto the wagon to sing for Josie's guests. Yet knowing that Logan had been listening from afar suddenly made her feel self-conscious. "Thank you. I don't really want to be known as a wedding singer, but I couldn't turn Josie down."

"You were better than good," Kinley said with a shake of her head toward her brother. "You mentioned once that you studied music in school?"

Alexis nodded. "I earned a master's in music from the Johns Hopkins Peabody Institute."

"Wow," Kinley said simply.

A quick crease of his eyebrows was Logan's only outward reaction, but still she could tell she had surprised him. "But you decided to plan weddings, instead."

It wasn't a question, since the answer was obvious. Still, she could tell he didn't really understand the path that had brought her here. She answered lightly, making sure she addressed her reply to both siblings. "You should both know by now that I like being in charge. I didn't get that when I was scrambling from one audition to another in New York, trying to get in enough hours at the florist shop to pay the rent. I'm much happier being my own boss—while still making my clients happy, of course. I've combined my training in stagecraft and performance with my experience in the floral shops to organize memorable weddings and other events, and I think it's all worked out very well."

"You're a very talented wedding planner," Kinley said immediately, then asked curiously, "When you say auditions…did you perform in New York? Like, on Broadway?"

Increasingly uncomfortable with discussing her past in front of Logan and trying at the same time to hide her connection to him from his sister, Alexis laughed softly. "More usually in choruses off-Broadway. Or off-off-Broadway. Needless to say, there are thousands of talented singers in New York waiting tables and working retail and arranging flowers. I guess I just didn't have the fierce drive necessary to climb over them all to the top."

Logan studied her face while Kinley voiced the question they were both probably thinking. "You don't miss the spotlight?"

It rather surprised her how long she hesitated before answering, "No, not really."

Shaking her head, she glanced at her watch, realizing how dim the light had become. "I should be going. Again, thank you both for another great collaboration."

Kinley patted her arm. "You, too, Alexis. Maybe we can do lunch someday soon. Sometime before the next event, perhaps."

"Lunch sounds nice. I'll be out of town at a seminar most of this week," she said without looking at Logan, "but I'll call you sometime after I get back to set up a time."

"I'd like that."

Alexis then glanced at Logan. "Thank you again for all your hard work, Logan. And please extend my appreciation to your crew."

He nodded. "I'll do that. Bye, Alexis."

She couldn't seem to return the goodbye. She merely smiled and turned away, instead.

Alexis opened her front door early Sunday evening and immediately found her arms filled with wiggling, whining dog, her face being bathed by an eager tongue. Staggering backward, she laughed, turned her face to one side to avoid having doggy kisses land on her mouth and fended him off. "Hello to you, too, Ninja."

Sighing in exasperation, Logan hauled his dog off her. "Ninja, down! Down."

The dog responded immediately to his owner's stern tone, but he didn't look notably abashed when he dropped to all fours. Tail wagging, he ambled over to the couch, where his feline friend waited to greet him with purrs and head butts.

"Sorry," Logan said as he entered. "I try to teach him manners, but he has very selective memory."

"He just knows when it comes to me, all he has to do is give me one of those goofy grins and I'll forgive him anything."

"You spoil him."

"Probably. But he's just so cute."

"And he knows it." With a lazy chuckle, he toyed with a lock of her hair. "I'd kiss you hello, but you have dog spit all over your face."

She laughed and playfully punched his arm. "Watch it, pal. You aren't quite as cute as Ninja."

Despite his teasing, he brushed a smiling kiss across her mouth, then raised an arm to display the brown paper bag dangling from his hand. "As promised, I brought dinner."

He'd texted earlier with an offer to bring take-out Chinese food, and though she'd had several chores to take care of this evening, she'd told him to come on over. She didn't always drop everything when Logan called; more than once she'd told him it wasn't a good time. But she'd wanted to see him tonight. After all, she'd be leaving for Seattle in a few days and she'd be hectically busy after she returned. And she had to eat, right?

Shaking her head in response to her own convoluted reasoning, she waved a hand toward the kitchen. "I just need to put a load of laundry in the dryer and then I'll be ready to eat."

"I'll set the table."

"Thanks. There's wine in the fridge. I chilled the Riesling you like."

"Sounds good." Unerringly, he opened the cabinet

that held her plates. As she stepped into the laundry room, which opened off the kitchen, it occurred to her that Logan had become very familiar with her house. He was as at home in her kitchen as in her bedroom.

When had that happened, exactly? He hadn't been here that many times, had he? She did a quick mental count and was rather surprised by the estimated number she reached. What had started out as an occasional hookup was on the verge of becoming habit.

She should probably do something about that. Later.

Chapter Five

Still distracted by her wandering thoughts about Logan, Alexis opened the lid of her aging washing machine, then groaned when she saw her clothes still sitting in a tub of water.

"Problem?" Logan asked from the doorway.

"It didn't drain."

"Here, let me take a look."

Sighing, she stood back while Logan moved past her. "Looks like a broken drive belt," he said a couple minutes later. "Is the machine yours or provided in your rent?"

"The washer and dryer are mine, so I'm responsible for their maintenance. I'll have to call a repairman tomorrow."

"No need for that. None of the appliance parts stores are open on Sunday evening, but I can pick up a belt for you tomorrow. I'll come by tomorrow night to put it on."

She shook her head. "There's no reason for you to go to all that trouble. I'll just call a repairman first thing in the morning."

"Don't be ridiculous. This is what I do, remember? I fix things like this all the time around the inn. This isn't even a difficult repair. It'll take me maybe twenty minutes. But you know how much you'd have to pay a repairman just for the service call, not to mention parts and labor?"

"If it's that easy, maybe it's something I can do myself?"

Logan pushed a hand through his hair, beginning to frown. "Is there some reason you don't want me to fix your washing machine?"

She didn't have an answer—even for herself. Why *was* she so uncomfortable at the thought of having Logan help her with a repair? It was no big deal, right? Friends did this sort of thing for each other. She would lend him a hand with a problem if she could, wouldn't she? Had he not just happened to be here when she discovered the problem, she'd have handled it just fine on her own by calling a repairman, but of course Logan would offer to take care of it since, as he'd pointed out, this was what he did all the time.

"I just hate for you to go to all that trouble," she said lamely.

"No trouble. I'll write down the numbers from the machine, pick up the belt on the way over tomorrow and have you doing laundry half an hour after I get here."

"I'll reimburse you for the belt, of course." She almost added that she would also pay him for his time, but something told her that would only annoy him. "And dinner's on me tomorrow night."

He nodded, seeming to accept her excuse that she hadn't wanted to take advantage of him. "Let's eat before the food gets cold. I'll help you empty the washer afterward."

Pushing her complicated concerns to the back of her mind, she smiled rather tensely and turned back to the kitchen.

"Did you get everything cleared away from Josie's wedding?" she asked during the meal, retreating to the comfort of talking about their work.

"Yeah. There was a big retirement party in the dining room this afternoon and Kinley wanted all the decorations down beforehand so the party guests could walk through the gardens. We had all signs of the wedding gone last night."

"I know I've already told you, but the grounds really did look exceptionally nice yesterday. I wouldn't be at all surprised if we both get bookings as a result of that wedding."

"Thanks. Wish they were all that easy," he added pointedly.

She wrinkled her nose at him. "Let's not start that again."

Logan didn't smile, but concentrated on stirring the remains of his food aimlessly with his chopsticks as he looked at her. She couldn't read his expression, but found her gaze locked with his for several long moments. What was he thinking? It was so often hard to tell with him, but especially now.

He was the one who broke off the eye contact. He

pushed his nearly empty plate away. "We need to unload that washer so I can get the model number."

She'd finished her own dinner, so she stood and carried her plate to the sink, still feeling a little flustered by that tense moment between them. "I'll get a bucket and some plastic tumblers for bailing."

Fortunately, the washer held only three pairs of wet jeans, so she didn't have to wring out soggy underwear with him. She threw the jeans into a plastic laundry basket to deal with later, and then she and Logan bailed the standing water from the machine into a bucket that she emptied several times into the backyard. After he'd gotten the information he needed to buy the necessary belt, she turned off the laundry room light and closed the door, following him back into the kitchen.

"Would you like some more wine?" she asked.

He shook his head. "What I would like—"

However he might have finished that sentence, and she thought she knew, he was interrupted by a chime from his phone announcing a text message. He glanced down at the screen, then grimaced. "I have to go."

She tried to mask her disappointment behind concern. "Nothing serious, I hope?"

"One of the guests accidentally broke the bifold closet door in her room and now she can't open it. Bonnie said Paul would have tried to fix it, but I've got my tools locked up. I'd better go take care of it."

He gave her a firm kiss at the door that expressed his frustration at having to leave, and then he motioned Ninja to his side. Suddenly weary, Alexis sighed as she closed the door behind them. Her supposedly stress-

free, no-strings affair with Logan seemed to be growing more complicated. Maybe she'd been naive to have
thought it could stay easy and breezy. Logan was not
an easy man.

Logan kept an eye on his watch Monday afternoon.
He needed to leave early enough to stop by the appliance parts store on his way to Alexis's house. He'd
already called to order the belt, and had been promised it would be waiting for him.

He still didn't quite understand why Alexis had
been so hesitant for him to take care of this for her.
It would have been ridiculous for her to pay a repair
guy to make a twenty-minute house call to install a
fifteen-buck part. He knew she was the stubbornly
independent type—as she'd said herself, she liked
to be in charge—but what was the harm in letting a
friend lend a hand for something he knew how to do?

He had just put away his lawn-care tools for the
day when Bonnie came outside. "Did you remember
to order the new faucet for suite 3?"

He nodded. "It'll be in tomorrow."

"Good. Oh, by the way, I'm baking fish for dinner.
It will be ready to serve by six."

Though he didn't dine with them every evening, he
joined her and Paul often enough for meals that she
routinely prepared enough for him. "Sounds good,
thanks, but I already have plans for dinner tonight.
Actually, I have to leave shortly."

Bonnie's brows lifted in surprise. "Really? You're
going out again tonight?"

"Yeah. Why?"

"No reason," she assured him a bit too nonchalantly. "You've just been going out quite a bit lately."

He tugged one of her loose blond curls, speaking indulgently. "I'm getting all my homework done, Mom."

She laughed softly and leaned affectionately against him. "I'm not fussing. Just wondering if you're ever going to introduce us to this woman Kinley and I suspect you're seeing."

He kissed her forehead, then stepped away from her. "See you tomorrow, Bonnie."

"That's all you're going to say?"

"Yes."

She sighed heavily. "Fine. Have a good evening."

"I intend to."

Climbing into his truck, he wondered if he should feel guiltier that he and Alexis were deliberately misleading his sisters. By the time he'd driven as far as Bride Mountain Café—perhaps a quarter mile from his house—he'd decided he didn't feel at all guilty. Just picturing his well-intentioned sisters avidly watching them every time Alexis came to the inn for work made him wince. It would be different if they could just accept the relationship for what it was. He'd briefly dated a few other women in the past few years, and his sisters hadn't gotten carried away, not expecting him to settle down permanently with any of them. Something told him it would be different with Alexis.

It would be nice, he thought as he left the appliance store with the drive belt in hand, if he and Alexis could just see each other when they wanted to, maybe even go out in public together without everyone making a big deal of it. He wouldn't mind having dinner with her somewhere other than her kitchen. Preferably somewhere that there wouldn't even be a chance of them running into curious friends or clients. They'd taken a slight risk of exposure when they'd gone hiking last week, but it had been a calculated risk. They'd be somewhat more likely to be recognized at a local restaurant.

So maybe they should find a restaurant that wasn't local. One in a different city, entirely.

Say, Seattle, perhaps.

Alexis met him at the door with a slightly distracted smile. "I was just going over my lists," she admitted, nodding toward the tablet computer on the table. "My plane leaves at eleven tomorrow morning, and I'm always afraid I'll forget to pack something."

"Do you have a ride to the airport?"

"Yes, Gretchen's taking me. She'll be staying here at my house at night while I'm gone to take care of Fiona and keep an eye on things."

Shifting his tool bag in his left hand, he moved toward the laundry room. "I'll get your washer going so you can finish your laundry."

"I think I have everything important washed for now. What can I do to help you?"

"Stay out of my way. Go pack or fuss in the kitchen or whatever else you need to do and I'll have this done in a few minutes."

She was never offended by his bluntness, just another one of the many things he liked about her. "All right. I'll be in my room packing if you need me."

As he'd assured her, he changed the belt quickly and efficiently. The machine had an easy-access panel, so it wasn't a particularly complicated job. He checked his work, tightened everything else in the older machine that seemed to need attention, plugged it back in and made sure it worked as intended, then replaced his tools in the bag. A broom stood in the corner of the little laundry room; he swept the floor quickly to make sure he left it clean. Standing the broom back into place, he frowned suddenly, realizing how domestic this all seemed. He was certainly at ease in Alexis's house, increasingly familiar with her things, her tastes.

Shaking off that thought, he dropped his tool bag in the living room and went looking for Alexis. He found her in her bedroom, an open suitcase on the bed, piles of clothes stacked neatly around it. Her tablet computer lay close at hand. Knowing her so well, he was quite sure she had a comprehensive list of everything she needed to pack displayed on the screen.

Seeing that she was folding what looked suspiciously like a flame-red silk-and-lace nightgown, he frowned. It occurred to him that he'd never actually seen her in a nightgown. She was usually in street clothes when he arrived and often wrapped in a robe when he left. Though he told himself it was none of his business, he couldn't help wondering if some other guy would see her in that red thing in Seattle.

"The washer's fixed," he said abruptly.

It was obvious she hadn't seen him standing there when she started in response to his voice. She dropped the nightgown into the suitcase. "That was quick. No problems, I take it?"

"No. Easy job. How's the packing coming?"

"I've finally made myself put away everything I

don't really need to take," she replied with a laugh. "I'm a notorious overpacker."

He didn't want to talk about her trip. Instead, he headed across the room, his gaze fixed intently on the sweet curve of her lips.

Her smile faded in response to the look on his face. "Um—"

He lifted her into his arms and planted his mouth on hers. Though he'd given her no warning, she reacted immediately, wrapping her arms around his neck, her legs around his waist, returning the kiss with enthusiasm. His entire body seemed to harden in response to her eager welcome.

He took a step forward so that she was partially sitting on the top of her heavy, light-toned wood dresser, steadying herself with her arms on his shoulders. With her weight supported, his hands were free to roam and explore. Dropping her glasses onto the dresser out of the way, he slid his palms beneath her loose knit top, caressing her warm back, shaping her narrow waist, easing around to lift and cup her firm breasts through the bra that covered them. She murmured into his mouth when his thumbs pressed, circled, pushed aside lace to bare the taut tips to his ministrations.

Crowding closer to her, he swept the inside of her mouth with his tongue and she welcomed him hungrily. Still gripping his shoulder with one hand, she used the other to tug impatiently at the hem of his T-shirt, pulling it up over abs and pecs, getting tangled at his chin until he finally released her mouth long enough to sweep the shirt up, off and out of the way. She sighed with an appreciation that stoked his ego even higher as she ran her hands slowly over his chest.

Her shirt joined his on the floor, followed almost immediately by her bra. Both gasped when skin pressed to skin. Would being with her ever not make his head spin? Shouldn't familiarity have lessened the wonder at least marginally by now?

Jeans hit the floor. Hers, then his. Undergarments followed, tossed carelessly aside. Something from the dresser fell to the floor with a thud, but there was no crash of broken glass so he didn't bother to look down. His attention was focused solely on the naked, willing woman in his arms. Sliding a hand up her soft thigh, he wrapped her leg around him again, then surged forward. Alexis cried out softly in pleasure when he thrust into her tight heat.

This, he thought with a last moment of coherence, was exactly where he wanted to be.

She wore her robe during the dinner she'd made for them, a beef stew she'd cooked for several hours in a slow cooker. The food was good, but he ate rather perfunctorily. They didn't talk much during the meal, and when they did they confined their remarks to innocuous work chat. He stayed long enough afterward to help her clear away the dishes, then moved toward the living room to collect his tool bag.

Fiona butted against his leg, meowing, and he reached down to pet her. Even though she would have a sitter, Fiona was going to miss Alexis this week.

"It'll only be a few days," he murmured to the cat beneath his breath. "She'll be back before you know it. It'll probably be good for you to take a little break from each other."

Alexis appeared in the doorway, wiping her hands on a kitchen towel. She looked really good in her soft red robe. He tried not to picture her in a thin red column of silk and lace. "Did you say something?"

He straightened. "Just talking to the cat. I'd better clear out and let you finish packing. Is there anything else I can do for you before I go?"

She shook her head with a somewhat forced-looking smile. "Not that I can think of. Thank you again for fixing my washer."

She had already thanked him repeatedly and insisted on repaying him for the belt, though he'd told her to forget it. "You're welcome. So, uh—have a good time in Seattle."

But not too good, he wanted to add, but didn't because they didn't express that sort of wayward thought to each other.

"Thank you. Do you have any fun plans for while I'm gone? Did you set up a fishing-and-beer outing with your friends?"

He shrugged. "No. I've got an invitation to a party Friday night, but I haven't given an answer yet."

"Oh. Well…um, have a good time, and I'll see you when I see you."

They were both stammering more than usual tonight. Shaking his head, he turned toward the door. "Good night, Alexis."

It occurred to him only when he was in his truck and halfway up Bride Mountain that he hadn't kissed her good-night. Perhaps subconsciously he'd been afraid he wouldn't want to leave if he did.

* * *

Logan didn't sleep well that night. Nothing new for him—he didn't require a lot of sleep. He gave up at 4:00 a.m., made a pot of coffee and sat at the computer, figuring he might as well work here until it was light enough to busy himself around the grounds. Accustomed to his master's odd hours, Ninja made a quick trip outside, then returned to curl at Logan's feet to finish his snooze.

For an hour, Logan concentrated fiercely on work, though his restless mind tried occasionally to distract him with fleeting images of a pretty brunette in a red silk nightie. Saving a file, he stretched, checked his email, then impulsively did a search for photos of Seattle. Looked like a nice place, though he read a few comments about March being an iffy time to visit. He checked the five-day forecast for Seattle and noted that it didn't look too bad. For Alexis's sake, he hoped the weather cooperated for her there. She deserved a good time on the short vacation she was taking after her seminar ended, and he wasn't sure how much fun she could have closed up in a hotel room by herself on a rainy day. Now if she had company in that room, a very good time could be had, indeed.

He shook his head impatiently and called up a website from which he ordered landscaping supplies. He could arrange a shipment for later this week—or maybe early next week, if he wanted to take a few days off beforehand. It was an ideal week to get away, giving him a break from routine. Besides, there was a reception scheduled this weekend that he'd rather have multiple root canals than attend. He could take a camping hike to avoid it, maybe. Or a fishing trip.

Or a flight across the country.

He told himself it was only idle curiosity that had him checking the price of airfare from Virginia to Washington. He choked a little in response to the numbers that popped up on his screen. Last-minute fares were expensive. If ever he decided to take a trip like that, he really should plan in advance. Of course, he didn't spend a lot day to day. His needs were few, his tastes rather simple. He could justify an occasional splurge.

What would be the consequences if he decided to join Alexis in Seattle? Would they return refreshed and satisfied, ready to dive back into their jobs, content with the stolen time they'd spent together even if there was little spare time to see each other in coming months? Or would he find that he'd grown even more accustomed to being with her, that he would miss her when he wasn't with her, would be less content in the solitude of his cozy cottage? Wasn't that exactly what he'd tried to avoid from the beginning with her?

Would he be an idiot to spend time with her there and take the risk of future dissatisfaction? Or would it be foolish of him to give up a chance to experience one probably enjoyable private weekend with her before the start of busy season and perhaps the end of the affair? He was, after all, in charge of his own emotions. His scarred heart was well guarded. Still, he was a healthy, red-blooded man with needs and appetites and he'd never seen Seattle....

Ninja whined and rested his head on Logan's knee, looking from the computer screen to Logan's face and back again.

He looked down at his dog with a shake of his head.

"Yes, I know what you would do. You do realize, of course, that I wouldn't take you with me? You'd have to stay here, with Bonnie and Paul and the others."

Ninja sighed heavily, but his tail wagged slowly against the floor. Logan gave a short laugh and rubbed the dog's ears. "I've been listening to my sisters and Alexis too much. They've got me having conversations with you and thinking you're answering me."

The dog stood, wandered over to his water bowl and began to lap noisily. Logan turned back to his computer, rather wishing his canine friend could offer some sage advice.

The seminar was as useful and informative as Alexis had hoped it would be. She learned a lot, made some good connections, considered it an investment well spent. Busy with workshops and networking, she hardly left the hotel during the seminar, which ran from early Wednesday morning until noon on Thursday. She figured she had time to explore afterward, before her plane left Sunday.

What little she had seen from the cab and from the balcony of her room had looked intriguing, if rather gray. The locals had informed her that it had been a nice March thus far. Misty, of course, as was typical of Seattle before the beautiful summer weather set in, but temperatures had ranged from the mid-fifties to the low sixties and the sun peeked through the clouds occasionally. She looked forward to checking out some of the local attractions that had been recommended to her.

She would be exploring the city on her own. She didn't mind eating or exploring alone, but it would have been nice to have a sightseeing companion. Not just any companion, of course. She probably could have found a friendly tour guide among the local wedding planners who'd presented talks during the seminar. A rather attractive videographer had hinted that he wouldn't mind spending time with her outside of shop talk. Alexis had let the hints pass unanswered. She wasn't interested in a seminar hookup. There was only one person she had wanted to join her in her very nice room, and he hadn't been interested.

Okay, she thought, taking a lined, hooded rain jacket from the closet in her room Thursday afternoon, maybe that was overstating things a bit. Logan had been interested. She'd seen the flicker of heat in his eyes when she'd mentioned the chance to share a room for a couple of days—and nights. Wariness had overpowered temptation, a battle she understood, as she'd had her own hesitations about taking that potentially relationship-changing step. Still, it might have been nice. She thought they could have handled it without unpleasant repercussions, considering they'd both been very clear about what they wanted—and didn't want—from each other.

Had Logan thought she'd been trying to change the rules by issuing the invitation to join her here? If that had been his concern, he must not know her as well as she'd thought he did.

Looping a cross-body bag over her right shoulder to hang at her left hip, she donned her rain jacket over her thin sweater and knit pants. Pike Place Market was only a few blocks from the hotel. She looked forward to seeing it.

The elevator doors opened to a big, airy lobby with

reception desks at one end and a casual bar at the other. Maybe she'd been thinking too much about Logan, she thought wryly. The dark-haired man standing at the reception desk in jeans and a gray jacket looked very much like him. He stood with his back to her, a navy duffel bag clutched in one hand. And when a clerk motioned him toward the desk, he moved with a slight limp of his left leg.

Her heart seemed to stop, then kick hard into rhythm again. She moved quickly in that direction. "Logan?"

He turned in response to her voice and held up the phone in his hand. "Hey. Nice timing. I was just about to send you a text."

"You're here," she said blankly. Unnecessarily.

His eyes were shadowed, his smile just a little crooked. "Yeah. Still got a place for me to stay while I'm here?"

She swallowed hard, then smiled and nodded. "There's a really big bed in my room."

He shifted the bag in his hand. "Sounds good to me."

Chapter Six

Logan dropped his bag onto the floor at the foot of the large bed in her room, his gaze taking in the two armchairs flanking a small round table, the flat-screen TV, the desk and chair in one corner, and the big glass door leading out onto a balcony overlooking Elliott Bay. "Nice room."

"Total splurge," she admitted. "I thought about moving to a less expensive place when the seminar ended, but it's just so nice here, I decided to go for it. I'll eat peanut butter and jelly for a couple months to make up for it."

He chuckled. "I'll pay for my part while I'm here. Maybe you'll only have to eat the PBJ for a month."

"I was so surprised to see you downstairs," she admitted, shaking her head in lingering disbelief. She'd been so certain he wouldn't come.

"I hope it was a good surprise. I know I should have let you know I was coming, but I sort of waited until the last minute to make up my mind."

She suspected his mental debate had been a hard-fought one. "It was a very nice surprise."

He pushed a hand through his hair. "You don't have any plans with anyone else for the rest of your stay? New friends from the seminar, maybe?"

"I met some very nice people during the seminar, but I made no plans with any of them."

He nodded. Did she see relief in his eyes? It was so hard to tell with him. "Have you done anything fun since you've been here?"

"It was a great seminar, but I've hardly left the hotel. I'm really looking forward to getting out and exploring."

"Sounds good to me." He moved to the window and looked out at the gray sky spread over the waterfront across the way. "Kind of cloudy."

She laughed softly. "It's Seattle. I'm told that as long as there isn't an outright downpour, this is considered a nice day in March."

"I looked up the weather before I packed. Sounds like the weekend is supposed to be decent."

Rapidly recovering from her surprise at finding him in the lobby, she dropped onto the foot of the bed, leaning back to support herself on her arms. "Even if it rains buckets, I'm sure we can find some way to entertain ourselves."

His mouth quirked into a half smile even as a spark ignited in his eyes. "You think?"

She patted the bed with one hand.

He looked tempted, but shook his head. "If you want to leave this room today, we'd better go now."

She debated a moment, then stood again. "I really would like to see the market."

"Besides," he said, "I'm starving. I left Virginia at six a.m. and my stomach thinks it's three hours later than that clock on the nightstand says it is."

She held out her hand to him. "Then let's go find you some food."

Lacing his fingers with hers, he smiled down at her. "But I will definitely want to try out that bed later."

Winking, she said, "You're on."

Even on a gray Thursday afternoon, the streets of downtown were packed with cars and buses and bicycles and Prius cabs. The longtime landmark Pike Place Market was crowded and noisy. They held hands to keep from being separated as they made their way past "Rachel," the bronze piggy bank sculpture at the entrance of the market, and into the crowd, watching fishmongers shouting jokes and tossing big, shiny silver fish through the air. They passed rows of fresh produce and colorful flowers, and booths of handmade jewelry, bags, soaps, lotions, candles and decor items. There were shops of teas, baked goods, gourmet foods, souvenirs, clothing and too many other items for Alexis to identify on an initial pass-through, and several levels of shops below the ground floor she would love to explore, but she knew Logan wanted to eat first.

They decided to dine at a popular brewery restaurant located within the market. Because she'd already eaten a light lunch, she ordered a small crab chowder while Logan selected a heartier meal of fish and chips and a house ale. She was rather amused by how eagerly he tucked in to the food when it arrived. He really was hungry.

"It's a long trip all the way across the country," he said with a slight smile when he noticed her watching him.

"It is," she agreed. "I was really tired by the time I got here Tuesday."

"I'm not particularly tired, just needed refueling. This halibut is good. So's the ale."

She smiled across the table at him. Around them, servers bustled, diners chattered, a child whined from a far corner, but as far as she was concerned, they could have been the only ones in the place. It was nice to be able to share a meal in public, to walk openly hand in hand, to have just a few days to enjoy each other without outside distractions. "I'm glad you came. What made you change your mind?"

He shrugged. "Like you said, I needed a break. Besides, Bonnie and Kinley are hosting a luncheon Saturday for a group of travel agents. You know, one of those networking things. I didn't want to be anywhere near it."

"Yes, I know about networking things," she murmured with a smile, thinking back over the past few days. "So...you have a travel-agent phobia or something?"

"Cute." He took another sip of his ale, then said, "If I were there, I'd probably be expected to make an appearance and schmooze for business. That's Kinley's thing, not mine. Besides, I, uh—"

She raised her eyebrows in question. "Yes?"

Blowing out a breath, he shook his head curtly. "I went out a couple of times with one of the women who are going to be there, back when we first re-opened the inn."

"Oh." She dipped her spoon into the remains of her chowder, letting the soup trickle back into the bowl. "Bad ending?"

He shrugged. "Turned out she was the kind who's always looking for a makeover project. I'm not the type who enjoys being made over."

"No, I wouldn't think so," she murmured into her coffee cup.

He jerked his chin in a short, dismissive gesture. "Mostly, I just wanted to get away for a couple days. The more I thought about it, the more I liked the sound of your offer."

Perhaps it wasn't the most flattering explanation, but it was so typically Logan. And because she liked him just the way he was, she had no desire to do a "makeover" on him.

"What did you tell your sisters?"

"That I was taking off for a few days. Didn't tell them where, and they didn't ask. They know they can reach me on my cell if they need me."

She thought again that he had an interesting rela-tionship with his sisters. "I suppose Bonnie is pleased that you took her advice about a vacation."

"Said she was. To be honest, she probably thinks I've got someone with me, but she won't ask who it is."

That worked just fine for Alexis.

"So, did you save room for dessert?" their server asked as he approached to remove their dishes. "We've got a hazelnut brownie that will make you weep."

Both Logan and Alexis declined the dessert. Alexis was eager to explore the waterfront, and now that he'd eaten, Logan was agreeable to sightseeing. They wandered through the market awhile longer, then down the wide concrete steps descending to the shops and attractions lining Elliott Bay. The Great Wheel, a giant Ferris wheel with forty-two dangling gondolas, towered 175 feet above them at the end of a pier, drawing their eyes up to the sky as they ambled along the waterfront sidewalk. They stopped to admire the variety of boats crowded into marinas, and to watch the ferries and water taxis chugging across the gray waters of Puget Sound toward the surrounding islands and beaches. They passed an aquarium, restaurants, curiosity shops and an arcade, but they stopped only a few times, mostly in the shops that drew Alexis's interest. Logan seemed content just to stroll and take in the scenery.

The clouds had parted to reveal the snowcapped Olympic Mountains against the western sky. Turning her back to the water, Alexis gazed up at the business, retail and residential skyscrapers that made up the downtown Seattle skyline. Turning north, she saw the iconic Space Needle peeking through an opening between buildings. She pointed it out to Logan, adding that she wanted to visit there, too.

"Now?" he asked, sounding game.

She smiled. "Maybe tomorrow. Let's just stay downtown this evening."

They had the next two days to play tourist, she thought happily.

They paused in front of a sign that offered tours of the underground city beneath Pioneer Square—storefronts, sidewalks and roadways that had been abandoned when the Great Seattle Fire of 1889 had destroyed much of what had then been a muddy, flood-prone downtown. While planning her activities, Alexis had read about the tours during a lull in the seminar, and she related what she'd learned to Logan now. When the city rebuilt, the streets and sidewalks had been raised and second stories became ground level. The lower level had been completely abandoned by 1907. Tours through the subterranean passages were now quite popular with visitors, who were regaled with tall tales of Seattle's sometimes seamy history along the way.

"Sounds interesting," Logan said. "I like unusual history stuff. I'm sort of a museum nerd."

"Really?" She cocked her head to look up at him in interest. "I didn't know that."

Smiling indolently, he tapped a fingertip against the end of her nose. "There's a lot you don't know about me."

Though he spoke teasingly, she was all too aware of how true that was.

She looked at the sign again. "The last tour is at six. We should be able to make it, if you want to go."

"Works for me." He kept his tone casual, but she could tell he liked the idea.

"Let's do it, then. Who knows, maybe we'll see a ghost or two down in those creepy passages," she said with a laugh, waving toward a poster advertising Seattle ghost walks.

She'd spoken without thinking of the old legend attached to Bride Mountain Inn, but his sudden grimace reminded her of his reluctance to acknowledge his own home's spooky tale. "Or maybe not."

He grunted. "No such thing as ghosts."

"Of course not. But sometimes it's sort of fun to pretend?"

His shuttered gaze tracing the path of a ferry chugging toward Bainbridge Island, he shrugged. "Generally, I find it best to stay grounded in reality. I believe in looking at life the way it is rather than the way you wish it was. Hoping to see something that isn't there is only going to lead to disappointment."

If he was trying to be subtle, he wasn't doing it very well, she thought with a slight shake of her head. But then, Logan wasn't known for his subtlety. Should she tell him outright he needn't worry that she'd misinterpreted his last-minute decision to join her here in Seattle? That she still saw their relationship for what it was—what they both wanted it to be?

"I've never been one to mix up fiction with reality," she replied instead. "I can enjoy happy-ever-after books and movies and whimsical ghost tours occasionally without deluding myself that they're real." And she could savor a stolen weekend without misconstruing it as a step toward the sort of "Great Romance" neither she nor Logan believed in, she almost added—but decided there was no need to oversell her point. Logan was a smart guy. He could read between the lines.

His nod of satisfaction told her he'd heard her correctly. "Let's go learn some history," he said, his tone lighter again.

With a smile that felt a little forced, she turned with him toward the stairs leading up to the city streets.

It was only 9:00 p.m. by the time they returned to the hotel room. The bars, clubs and restaurants of downtown Seattle were still open and active, but they weren't tempted to stay out later. For one thing, Logan was still operating on Eastern time. Besides which, as nice as it had been to be out in public without concern about running into people they knew, they were ready to be alone again.

Logan headed straight for the shower, saying he felt grubby after a day of travel and tourism. While she listened to the shower run, Alexis swapped her street clothes for the slinky red nightgown she'd packed and hadn't yet worn. Had she hoped even as she'd folded it into her bag that Logan would join her? She hadn't envisioned herself wearing it for anyone else.

She brushed out her hair to let it fall straight to her shoulders, then made a quick assessment of her appearance when she heard the shower stop. The thin silk clung where it should, draped softly over curves to pool around her feet. Tiny spaghetti straps bared her shoulders and arms, and a bodice of red lace concealed only slightly more than it revealed. She'd bought the gown on impulse a couple months ago. And maybe she'd thought of Logan when she purchased it.

He emerged from the bathroom wearing the white terry-cloth hotel robe that had been hanging on a door hook. He'd towel-dried his hair so that it was still damp, finger-combed back from his freshly shaven face. He stopped short when he saw her standing by the big dresser in her nightgown. She set down her hairbrush, her hand suddenly a bit unsteady in response to the look on his face.

"I was hoping you'd wear that," he said, his voice deeper, gruffer than usual. "I saw you pack it."

She smiled faintly. "Is that why you came? To see me in this nightie?"

"No." He took a step toward her, reaching out for her. "To take it off of you."

Her breathless laugh was smothered by his hungry kiss.

It was still dark in the room when the insistent buzz of Logan's phone on the nightstand startled them both out of deep sleep. Alexis focused blurrily on the clock as he groped for the phone, cursing beneath his breath. Six o'clock. After a deliciously energetic night, she'd rather hoped to sleep in this morning.

"What?" Logan barked into the phone. "Yes, I was. What do you need?…It's in the storeroom of my garage, third shelf down on the right….Yeah, no problem. But don't call again unless it's an emergency, got it? I'm trying to take a vacation."

He disconnected the call without a goodbye, then dropped the phone onto the nightstand again. "I should just turn the damned thing off."

"They need to be able to contact you if there is an emergency," she reminded him as she climbed from the bed, smoothing her tangled nightgown around her while she walked toward the bathroom. "But I'm sure whoever just called got the message that you don't want to be disturbed unless it's necessary."

"It was Curtis. I left him in charge of the grounds. Which means I expect him to handle things without calling me at the crack of dawn," he growled.

Curtis had no way of knowing, of course, that it was the crack of dawn for his boss, since Logan hadn't told anyone which time zone he was vacationing in.

She stopped to look outside on the way back to the bed a few minutes later. It was still an hour or so before sunrise, so the streets below were dark. Lights glowed on the waterfront and across the sound in West Seattle and Bainbridge Island. A light rain fell, blurring those lights and splashing against the balcony on the other side of the glass door. She tugged the drapes back into place and turned toward the bed again.

Logan watched her from his pillows. "Sorry about the early call. I hope you can go back to sleep."

She slipped beneath the covers and snuggled into his bare shoulder. "I'm in no hurry to get out of this bed. It's ridiculously comfortable, isn't it?"

Smoothing her hair from her face, he brushed his lips against her forehead. "Mmm."

She smiled against his warm skin. From her observations, Logan wasn't one to indulge in pillow talk. Of course, she hadn't spent that much time in bed with him. He never stayed long after their lovemaking at home. It was a new experience to sleep beside him, to wake with him—and it was nice. They had only two more mornings to wake together in the foreseeable future, and she would savor each moment to mentally replay in her solitary bed at home. Vacations were meant to be enjoyed and appreciated, though they couldn't last forever.

The room was considerably lighter when they woke again. Still, it took them a while to dress for the day, since Logan informed her gravely that she needed help washing her back in the shower. After a moment's consideration, she replied that there was, in fact, a spot she had trouble reaching by herself. The nightie hit the floor again when he stepped forward eagerly to offer his assistance.

Finally dressed for the day in clothes comfortable enough for a considerable amount of walking and sightseeing, she opened the curtains again to see if it was still raining. She gasped in pleasure when she gazed out. "Logan, look. The sun's out. It's so pretty."

He stepped up behind her, resting his hands loosely on her shoulders. Though soft gray clouds drifted across the sky, the midmorning sun beamed down on the waterfront and the sound, on the milling tourists and cruising ferries, on the soaring white-topped Olympic Mountains.

"There's Mount Rainier," she said, pointing to the horizon. "It's the first time since I arrived that I've been able to see it so clearly. Suddenly it looks so big and so close, but I know it's a couple hours away by car. Some of the locals at the seminar were talking about how pretty it is to hike up the mountain in the summer. They said the wildflowers are breathtaking."

"Sounds like a hike we'd like."

She nodded a bit wistfully. "Yes, it does."

"Maybe we'll try it sometime."

A jolt of nerves had her moving away from him, speaking with a brisk laugh. "Like either of us could slip away for several days during the summer months. We'd be lucky to manage another half-day hike in Virginia."

He was silent for a moment and she wondered if he regretted his random comment that implied a future between them. She was sure it had simply been a thoughtless contribution to the conversation. She shouldn't take it to mean anything more, so there was no need for her to be so jittery all of a sudden.

Still, she found herself talking a bit too quickly and too brightly. "I don't know about you, but I'm ready for breakfast. There's a great little place around the corner from the hotel where I had breakfast my first morning here. Delicious pastries and omelets. And the coffee— Well, it's Seattle. Coffee is serious business here."

Though he studied her face rather intently, he smiled a little when he responded. "Breakfast sounds good, but coffee sounds even better. I'm ready when you are."

She donned her jacket, grabbed her bag and phone, and moved toward the door, hardly waiting to make sure he was following. She couldn't have explained why she was suddenly so rattled. Silly, of course. Maybe it was just the whole adjustment to the novelty of sleeping with him, waking up with him, sharing a bathroom—things that took their relationship to an intimate new level, even if only temporarily.

A couple more days of fun and then they'd be back home, immersed in those busy schedules she'd just reminded him of. Rested, refreshed, ready to get back to work after the brief vacation they had both needed. She shouldn't waste the weekend trying to analyze his every word and expression, she decided, slowing her steps and smiling more naturally up at him. There was plenty of time after they returned to Virginia to decide how to proceed—if at all—with their affair.

Chapter Seven

It was immediately apparent that a beautiful spring day brought out the crowds in Seattle. While locals celebrated a respite from a long winter, tourists took advantage of the clear views of the Olympic Mountains to the west and the Cascades to the east, frantically snapping photos of Mount Rainier and the Space Needle from dozens of different angles.

With Logan indulgently tagging along, Alexis cheerfully played tourist along with everyone else, taking photos and standing in line to buy tickets for the monorail. The two-minute elevated ride took them to Seattle Center, where they admired the International Fountain, then rode the elevator to the top of the Space Needle for the breathtaking views of the mountains, the sound and the sprawling surrounding neighborhoods.

Logan didn't complain when she browsed gift shops full of souvenirs and local handicrafts, and he seemed to enjoy the music and science fiction museums. While she explored yet another gift shop, he fell into conversation with a security guard. Stuffing her purchase—a cheesy but cute little ceramic replica of the Space Needle—into her bag, she approached them just as the men shook hands and the guard moved on.

"That looked like a serious conversation."

Logan nodded. "We were talking about the best places to eat lunch around here."

"So where are we going?"

He chuckled. "Depends on what you're in the mood for. Pacific Northwest seafood, Thai, Vietnamese, Chinese, Japanese, Ethiopian, Greek, Indian, Korean, Mediterranean..."

She laughed and shook her head. "Maybe you should just pick one and surprise me."

After riding the monorail back downtown, they dined on Vietnamese food—stuffed escargot followed by pan-fried lemongrass sea bass for him, papaya salad and stir-fried vegetarian rice noodles for her. Logan had studied the menu carefully before making his selections, his expression so serious that she was rather amused. He'd done the same last night when they'd eaten at a popular seafood establishment, consulting with the server before ordering a wood-grilled chinook salmon dish that he declared "delicious."

"You really are a foodie, aren't you?" she asked him with a smile as she twirled noodles around her chopsticks. "Since we usually eat takeout or easy meals at my place, I didn't realize what an adventurous palate you have."

He looked a little self-conscious about her teasing. "I'm usually happy eating just regular stuff at home. I'm certainly no chef. Bonnie says I'd probably live on grilled steak and microwave-baked potatoes if she didn't invite me to dinner several times a week, and she's probably right. I guess I'm just in the habit of ordering more interesting dishes when I'm dining out and someone else is doing the cooking."

"You and I haven't really eaten out at home."

He shrugged. "Just seemed too likely we'd run into people we know."

"It wasn't a criticism. It was every bit as much my choice to stay in for the meals we've shared."

He nodded and glanced around the rather crowded dining room in which no one was in the least interested in them. "Still, it's kind of nice to be able to eat out together for a change."

"Yes, it is."

She sipped her green tea, then set the cup on the table. "I dined out all the time when I lived in New York. Trying new restaurants was something my group of friends did at least once a week. Since I've owned this business, unless I'm being served at an event, I find myself eating on the run, or just settling for something quick I can make at home and eat while I do the never-ending paperwork."

"I have lunch at the diner a couple times a week, and Bonnie has me to dinner fairly often, or I'll meet with some guys to watch a game over pizza and beer, but I fend for myself the rest of the time. Occasionally, when a new place opens, I like to check out the menu, either by myself or with friends."

She wondered how often those "friends" were actually dates. She knew he hadn't been seeing anyone else since they'd gotten together, but that had been only a few months and she doubted he'd been entirely celibate beforehand. Logan's healthy appetite was not limited to food. Perhaps he hadn't worried about being seen out and about with those other women, who weren't connected to him through their work and his sisters, leading to far fewer potential complications.

"You said your father introduced you to fine dining," she remarked, partially to distract herself from thoughts of those less-complicated women. "I'm sure with all his world travels, he's tried a lot of different foods."

Logan's expression went studiously blank, though his reply was cordial. "Yeah. He liked trying to gross us out when we were kids by telling us about the weird stuff he'd tried—scorpions and rattlesnakes and various animal organs. But mostly he enjoys traditional ethnic cuisines from various other countries. He talks a lot these days about New Zealand dishes— traditional Maori foods, Kiwi-Asian fusion, that sort of thing. Kinley said last time she talked to him, he mentioned that he's thinking about resettling again. He's looking at Bali."

"Bali, really? Intriguing choice."

Logan shrugged. "He has exotic interests."

"Have you ever visited him in any of those exotic countries?" She thought she already knew the answer, but she had to ask.

As she'd expected, he shook his head. "No. Only time I've ever left this country was to go hiking in British Columbia with some friends the summer after my first year of college. Had a great time."

Maybe he hoped she would be sidetracked to ask about his trip, but she was still trying to understand his relationship with his father. "Did your dad never invite you to join him?"

She thought she heard what might have been a faint sigh of resignation before he said, "Not really. Until I was in high school, his excuse was that I was too young. Then I got involved in sports, and I didn't want to miss the seasons, especially baseball in summer. Some other things came up while I was in college that kept me from traveling for a while. After I earned a degree, I got busy making a living, starting a software business, helping out Uncle Leo when I could. It just never worked out for me to take off to whatever distant location Dad had landed in. Now it just seems better to leave things the way they are."

She thought back to her brief meeting with Logan's father. She'd been at the inn with a potential client and Bonnie had introduced them when they'd passed in the hallway. Looking like an older, more grizzled version of his son, Robert Carmichael had been lean and sun-weathered, his manner gruff but pleasant.

He'd spoken to his daughters fondly but somewhat too jovially, and even at the time, Alexis had thought it was as if he didn't really know Bonnie and Kinley all that well, but was trying to hide the fact from outsiders. She hadn't seen him with Logan during that visit, so she had no idea what undercurrents she might have sensed if she had.

Remembering Logan's comment that seeing his dad over Christmas would hold them for a year or two, she thought it sad that they had such a distant connection. But then again, she'd had a difficult relationship with her own father, so she could relate to an extent.

"My dad stayed around after he and Mom divorced, but I wouldn't say we were all that close," she confided impulsively. "There were times I thought he saw me more as a weapon to use against my mom than as his daughter."

Logan grimaced. "Damn. That's rough."

Suddenly realizing what she'd said, she blinked in surprise. A short, humorless laugh escaped her as she shook her head. "Sorry, I don't think I've ever said that aloud before. Must be the green tea—I think it's going to my head."

It was a bad joke, and he made no effort to smile. "Acrimonious divorce, I take it?"

"Very. My brother and I were quite young and our parents fought several bitter custody battles during our childhood, making certain we knew all the angry details. We were never sure when they went to court who we'd end up living with, though Mom always ended up keeping primary custody with us seeing Dad on weekends and holidays. When we reached our teens, my brother ended up spending more time with Dad and I stayed with Mom. That seemed to satisfy both of them. Mom could live vicariously through my music and dance performances and Dad was free to push Sean toward a career in professional sports. I loved my dad, and I grieved when we lost him, but I can't say we were ever truly close."

"Your brother is an athlete?"

She shook her head. "No. He didn't have the self-discipline to work that hard at any one sport. He's a department manager in a sporting goods store now. Last I heard, he's considering pursuing professional bass fishing."

She touched her napkin to the corners of her mouth, then smiled wryly at Logan. "All this was just my way of letting you know I understand what it's like not to have a traditional relationship with your father."

Logan nodded. "At least we were spared the vicious custody battles. There was never any question that we would stay with Mom. And she never said a bad word about him. She claimed to love him until the day she died, she just said she couldn't live the nomadic way he did, especially after she had three kids in just over four years. She always made excuses for him—said he tried to stay in one place and be a responsible husband and father, but it was simply against his nature. That's bull, of course. He was just too selfish to make the effort. She made sure we talked to him often on the phone, and that we wrote him letters and sent photos, and she always welcomed him and accommodated him on his annual visits. If she had any bitterness or resentment over the way things worked out between them, she never even hinted at it to us."

"She sounds like a special woman."

"She was," Logan said, his voice deepening. "My sisters and I had a great childhood. We stayed in Tennessee because that was where my maternal grandmother settled when she remarried after losing her first husband in an industrial accident when my mother was a toddler. Mom wanted to be close to her mother and stepdad after her own marriage broke up.

Grandma had sold her share of the inn to her brother, Great-Uncle Leo, years earlier, but they remained close and Leo was an important part of my mom's childhood—as he was of ours. So we had Grandma and her husband to spoil us in Tennessee, and Uncle Leo and Aunt Helen indulging us every time we came to Virginia. I can't say we lacked for anything, really. The girls and I hardly remembered Dad ever living in the same household with us, so we didn't miss what we'd never had."

She believed him when he said his childhood had been a happy one. His still-close relationship with his sisters was ample testimony to that. Still, she suspected it hadn't been as easy as he implied to grow up without his father in his life, even though he and his sisters had adjusted to that reality from an early age. She thought there was still more about his past he hadn't told her—something that had left scars on his heart as well as his body. He had his reasons for being so solitary and cynical, and she didn't think she'd heard them all. But maybe they'd shared enough about their pasts.

"So, what would you like to do after lunch?" she asked brightly, taking out her handy tourist guide. "We could take a ferry over to Bainbridge Island and check out the galleries. Or we could ride a water taxi to Alki Beach and see the replica of the Statue of Liberty there. Or we could watch boats go through the locks from Lake Washington to Puget Sound and vice versa."

"I wouldn't mind visiting the locks," Logan said. "Unless you'd rather do one of those other things."

Watching boats, riding a ferry, strolling the streets—

it occurred to her that she didn't really care what they did, as long as they did it together. But maybe it would be best if they spent the rest of the time focusing on fun and not dwelling on their pasts.

He loved watching her laugh. Her whole face lit up, making her gray eyes gleam as silver as the water sparkling around them as they strolled through the grounds of the Hiram M. Chittenden Locks, which included a botanical garden. Alexis laughed quite a bit during their visit, proving she'd put their somber conversation about absentee fathers out of her mind for the afternoon, to Logan's approval.

The waning sun poked through gathering clouds, beams glittering in Alexis's hair, which she wore casually loose around her shoulders. Though the air was still chilly enough to make their jackets feel good, the sunlight had brought out quite a few Friday afternoon visitors to the complex. They gathered at the safety fences surrounding the locks, watching barges and tugs and yachts being raised to the lake or lowered to the sound below. At the highest level, the crew and passengers on the vessels were almost even with the spectators, nearly close enough to reach out and touch.

Logan wondered if the boaters felt a bit like zoo exhibits with so many curious eyes and lifted cameras aimed at them, but maybe they were used to the gaping, or simply too busy to be self-conscious. A few of them waved and returned greetings, but mostly they seemed eager to be on their way.

Beyond the two locks, he and Alexis and the other visitors crossed in front of a 235-foot spillway to reach the fish ladder incorporated into the far side. A steel sculpture shaped to look like curving silver waves dominated the pavement at the top of the ladder, and quite a few tourists posed for photos among the repetitive forms. From there, ramps led down to the underground viewing room. No fish jumped in the water that rushed down the twenty-one steps that made up the ladder. They'd been told they'd be lucky to see even one or two steelhead making use of the ladder this late in the migratory season.

Alexis was excited to spot a lone steelhead swimming lazily in the green water on the other side of the glass panels built into the wall of the underground fish viewing room. Stadium-style concrete benches faced the glass and large signs displayed drawings and information about the different types of salmon that could be observed at various times of the year.

"You should come back in the late summer or early fall sometime," an indulgent elderly man told her, seeing her pleasure at identifying the fish. "It's a lot of fun watching the big chinook and coho and sockeye salmon jumping up the ladder and crowding into this passage on their way through, sometimes so many of them they can hardly move."

Somehow Alexis ended up sitting on a bench beside the man, their heads bent over a cell phone filled with photographs he'd taken during his many visits here. Standing to one side to silently watch the interchange, Logan realized that Alexis wasn't just being polite. She was actually enjoying listening to the man's stories, and the old guy was lapping up the attention from the attractive younger woman.

She definitely had a way about her, a warmth that drew people to her. Her heart might be well guarded behind hard-earned barriers, but somehow she still came across as open and genuinely interested in others. It was no wonder she'd done so well with her business thus far. Her brides and other clients liked her, and they believed that she was sincerely interested in making them happy. Which was the truth. Despite the strife-filled youth she'd described to him earlier—or maybe because of that early chaos—she had emerged as a thoughtful, generous, outgoing adult. Perhaps ironically, he, who had experienced a happy, supportive, mostly carefree early childhood, was more prone to hiding himself away from people, even pushing them away, closing himself off.

Yet still something had drawn them together. And though he'd originally tried to brush it off as nothing more than a powerful physical attraction, he was increasingly certain there was more to it. He'd enjoyed hanging out with her here in Seattle, even outside the hotel room. He hadn't even minded too badly when they'd swapped personal revelations because frankly, he'd been interested in what he'd learned about her today. Not that he wanted to spend the rest of their vacation having heart-to-hearts about past pain, but the one conversation hadn't been as bad as he might have expected. Maybe that, too, just seemed safer here, away from their real lives.

Back above ground a short while later, they took their time crossing over the dam again, pausing to watch seagulls, herons, diving birds and the occasional jumping fish, and to observe the taller ships cruising beneath a railroad drawbridge on their way toward the locks from the sound. A sea lion entertained the spectators by randomly popping up and submerging in Salmon Bay, making younger visitors—and a few older ones—squeal and point whenever it emerged.

Alexis laughed again, the musical sound making his stomach tighten in response. She looked up at him and shook her head almost sheepishly. "I laugh every time he pops up, don't I? I don't know why I find it so funny. I only wish I could have seen salmon jumping like mad up the ladder, the way they were in Mr. Burroughs's photographs. I'm sure that's a lot of fun."

He draped an arm loosely around her shoulders. "It is rather dark humor, you know."

She turned with him in the direction of the exit gates. "What do you mean?"

"Well, I mean they're so darned focused on getting to a place where they'll just spawn and die. Sort of reminds me of some of the brides and grooms we've hosted at the inn."

She laughed again, though more ironically this time. "You would come up with something like that."

They crossed a narrow walkway over the first gate, staying to the right so people going the other direction could pass them—two young guys walking their bicycles, tourists with cameras hanging from their necks, a woman pushing a jogging stroller, a couple with two big dogs on leashes. Alexis had commented earlier that Seattle seemed to be a city full of dog lovers; everywhere they'd been during the past day and a half, they'd seen dogs on leashes and in carriers and even in doggy strollers, all breeds and sizes and colors.

"Ninja would love it here," she said now.

Logan looked up at a grassy hillside on which a flock of Canada geese milled and pecked. He pictured his dog making one of his notorious escapes from his leash and cheerfully dispersing the peaceful group. "Yeah. Not sure Seattle's ready for Ninja, though."

Alexis giggled and laced her fingers with his. She seemed to enjoy holding hands here, maybe just because they were free to do so. He wasn't complaining.

They passed the visitors center where they'd earlier watched a film about the history of the locks and browsed the gift shop. Alexis did have a weakness for gift shops, he thought with a slight smile. Though she'd been the first to declare it totally tacky, she'd been unable to resist buying a plastic fridge magnet shaped like a leaping salmon and printed with the locks logo.

They weren't quite ready to return to the hotel room, so they ate a leisurely dinner out, sharing crab-and-artichoke pizza this time. Afterward, they wandered into a downtown bar with live music, a very good three-piece combo, and were lucky enough to find a table even on this bustling Friday evening. Their table wasn't ideal, being located just off the main traffic pattern to the exit, but the service was good, as were the drinks and the music. They were even able to talk without raising their voices by sitting close together at the tiny table, so Logan wasn't complaining.

Alexis smiled at him, looking a little tired but content. "I've had a great day. It was so much fun playing tourist with you."

He reached out to brush her jaw with the backs of his fingers. "I had a good time, too."

"One more day and then we have to get back to work," she said with a low sigh. "What would you like to do tomorrow?"

He shrugged. "You can pick something from your handy tourist guide. I'm sure I'll like it."

She'd pored over that travel guide so much he figured she must have it memorized, and her spate of suggestions seemed to confirm that suspicion. "Maybe the art museum. And maybe one of the other cool museums in town, like the flight museum. One of the beach parks, if the weather is nice again. Or there's Green Lake or the zoo or a ferry ride to Bainbridge Island…or maybe you'd like to check out the Microsoft Visitor Center, being a computer geek yourself. Who knows? You could decide to join the huge tech community here."

Though he knew she was teasing, he shook his head. "I'm not looking for another computer job. I'm a groundskeeper these days, and perfectly happy with it."

She studied his face with her head tilted in curiosity. "Did you close your software company when you reopened the inn? What made you decide you'd rather be a groundskeeper than a full-time software designer?"

"It just worked out that way," he said offhandedly. "Actually, my business closed a few months before Uncle Leo died and left us the inn. Turned out the partner I thought I could trust was— Well, let's just call him a creative bookkeeper."

Her eyes widened in shock. "He embezzled from the business?"

"Not to the extent that he could be prosecuted. He covered himself legally, but he was definitely unethical about it. He pretty much cleaned us out, then took off, and I was the one left to make the choice of shutting down or going into big debt to start up again. Then my sisters and I inherited the inn and I decided to help them get it up and running again while I decided what to do next. Turns out keeping up the inn and working with my sisters suits me just fine. I like it. It means something to me to know I'm maintaining a place that's been in my mother's family for four generations. Doing the software consultations on the side lets me put my training and experience to use when I choose to, so I've got the best of both worlds."

Which was all he wanted to say for now about the fiasco with his former friend-slash-business-partner. "So, no computer stuff tomorrow. Let's just do the tourist thing."

"Museums, then," she said, taking his hint to change the subject. "And maybe a park if the weather cooperates. Green Lake Park looks nice in all the photographs."

"Whatever you want to do."

She laughed softly. "You're being very agreeable this evening."

Thinking of how nicely the day had started— waking up in bed with her—he shrugged. "As you said, it's been a good day."

She reached over to squeeze his left thigh beneath the table. Her thumb rested on his knee, only an inch or so above the knotted scar tissue that bracketed it. She'd never asked about those scars after the first time she'd seen him unclothed. She'd been satisfied with his terse explanation that he'd injured himself playing college sports and had apparently gotten the message that he didn't like to talk about it. Alexis always respected his privacy. Even though she'd asked more about his dad and his former business than usual today, he knew she'd have backed off either subject if he'd asked her to, just as she'd taken his cue to move on just now.

He hadn't exactly lied to her about his scars. He just hadn't told her everything. The malignancy in his leg had been discovered almost by chance when he'd broken his tibia playing an intramural rugby game at college. In his experience, people had a lot of different responses to hearing he'd battled cancer. Most of those reactions were ones he didn't want to see from Alexis.

To distract himself from those thoughts—and just because he wanted to—he leaned over to brush a kiss across her lips. She reached up to clutch his shirt, tugging him closer to make the kiss last just a little longer. Neither of them paid the least attention to the people drinking, talking and milling around them and even if anyone was looking at them, Logan couldn't care less.

Alexis was smiling when he lifted his head, and she looked as unconcerned as he was about any potential spectators.

"So, are you about done with that drink?" he asked, hearing the husky edge to his own voice. "Ready to head back to the room?"

She set down the almost-empty glass. "Actually, I am getting—"

"Alexis? Alexis Mosley? Oh, my gosh, I can't believe it!"

In response to her name, Alexis turned so fast she almost knocked her glass off the table. Logan reached out quickly to steady it before looking up.

The woman was tall, very slender except for im-

pressive breasts, very spray-tanned, very blonde.
Clothes too skimpy for the weather, heels too high for
walking more than a few feet. Jewelry jingled when
she bent to kiss the air at either side of Alexis's face.

"Isabella, what a nice surprise!" Alexis said, her
voice more artificially sparkling than Logan had ever
heard it. "It's been ages since we've seen each other."

"Oh, girl, I know. When was it? Two? Three years
ago?"

"Closer to three, I think. It must have been that
thing at Brayden's place."

"Oh, my God, that was wild, wasn't it? I'm pretty
sure my elbows are still purple."

Which made no sense to Logan at all, of course,
but Alexis laughed brightly. It didn't sound at all like
the easy laughter he'd heard from her earlier. "Crazy,"
she said. "So what are you doing in Seattle?"

"I'm in a show at the cutest little theater here. It's a
new play by an amazing young talent. Final rehears-
als this week, and opening night next weekend. Please
tell me you'll still be in town."

"I'm afraid not. I'm devastated."

"I'm heartbroken."

And I'm nauseated. Logan bit the inside of his
mouth, staying still and quiet so as not to draw attention to himself. Isabella had given him a quick once-
over and then turned away, obviously writing him off
as unimportant.

"I see Paloma occasionally," she said to Alexis.
"She's really making a name for herself these days.
Have you stayed in touch with her?"

"Yes, we're still quite close, though I haven't seen
her in a while."

"She looks great. I think she's had something done, though I can't figure out exactly what it was. Obviously, she's found a brilliant doctor. You should ask her next time you talk to her. Oh, and by the way, Jerry was asking about you a few weeks ago. He's getting some things together for early next year and he'd be thrilled to hear from you. You are going back to the city, aren't you?"

Alexis murmured something inaudible, then exchanged more smacking air kisses with Isabella, who rushed away immediately afterward.

Logan stared hard at Alexis when they were alone again. "Who the hell was that?"

"Isabella Larkins. We knew each other in New York. Sorry I didn't introduce you, but I thought—"

"I wasn't talking about *her,*" he interrupted. "I meant you. I've never seen you act quite like that."

Her face went pink in response to his comment, and he realized he'd displayed his usual lack of tact. But, damn. That had been a weird exchange.

"That was the New York Alexis," she muttered, looking down at her hands. "I'm not sure you'd have liked her. There were times I wasn't crazy about her myself."

He couldn't imagine not liking Alexis. But then, he'd rather be stabbed with a million sharp toothpicks than to mingle with the New York theater crowd. He remembered the way she'd hesitated before answering when Kinley had asked if she missed performing, though she'd ultimately replied that she did not.

Odd to think they never would have met if she hadn't decided to give up performing and start direct-

ing, in a way. They'd never really talked about what
had triggered that decision. But then, there were a lot
of things they'd never talked about.

Chapter Eight

Alexis tossed her bag onto the table in the room, which had been tidied and turned down during the hours they were gone. It had been a long day, she thought, replaying everything they'd seen and done during their adventures. Yet it had seemed to pass all too quickly, in some ways.

The room seemed particularly quiet after the busy day and the noisy club. She pushed a hand through her hair and turned to look at Logan, who'd fallen quiet again. "Who'd have thought I'd actually run into someone I know all the way on the other side of the country?" she asked wryly.

He shrugged and began to empty his pockets onto a nightstand. "Small world. I'd think that's especially true of the theater world."

"I guess. I don't see many of that crowd in Vir-

ginia, but I've been too busy with my business during
the past couple of years to spend time at the theater."

He nodded. "I don't see many associates from my
old software design days in Tennessee, either. Some
of them could have ended up here in Seattle, considering how many tech companies are located here, but
I'm not interested in reconnecting with any of them."

"Oh, I feel the same way," she assured him. "Isabella and I weren't really friends, simply acquaintances and occasional cast mates. We ran in the same
crowd, but we didn't have much in common otherwise."

"Who's the Paloma she mentioned?"

She sank onto one side of the bed to remove her
shoes. "Paloma Villarreal is my best friend from my
Peabody days. We went to New York together. She
stayed there, and she loves it. She's very talented,
makes a good living in the cast of a long-running musical and has had a few other offers she's considering."

"Sounds like you miss her."

"I do," she admitted. "We talk often, but that's not
quite the same as spending time together."

"So will you go back?" Sitting on the other side of
the bed with his back to her, he kicked off his shoes.
"To New York, I mean."

"To visit? Yes, probably, though I'm not sure when
I'll have the time. To live? No."

She glanced over her shoulder to see him unstrap-
ping his watch, which he then laid on the nightstand
with the former contents of his pocket. For a moment,
she was taken aback by how domestic the scene had
become. She was more accustomed to Logan sweeping her into his arms, tumbling her onto the bed as

soon as they were alone together. Was familiarity already breeding—well, not contempt, perhaps, but nonchalance? She'd known the passion wouldn't last, but she hadn't thought a day and a half of a joint vacation would dampen it so quickly.

Setting her glasses on the nightstand, she stood and started to walk toward the dresser to pull out her nightclothes. Before she'd made it halfway across the room, she was suddenly whirled around and lifted against him. His mouth was on hers, his hands sweeping her body. And the passion that she'd thought had dampened was suddenly ignited again, flaring through her so swiftly, so unexpectedly, that she felt the heat on her skin. One moment she was standing on her feet, the next she was lying on her back on the bed with Logan looming over her. She reached up to tug him down into the flames with her.

They had tonight, tomorrow, then one last night of this retreat to go. She'd be a fool not to make the most of it while it lasted.

She came awake slowly, reluctantly. She was so content and comfortable, snuggled into a soft bed, a warm shoulder. Keeping her eyes closed for a little longer, she focused on sounds—a soft rain against the window, a steady heartbeat beneath her ear. She moved her hand slightly and her fingers brushed against sleek, taut skin over firm, defined muscles. A strong arm wrapped around her, and a long leg tangled with hers. Maybe if she kept her eyes closed, she could make this perfect moment last just a while longer.

Logan brushed his lips against her forehead. "Playing possum?"

She nestled more deeply into him. "Mmm. Savoring."

"Thought you wanted to do museums this morning."

"Mmm-hmm. Maybe later."

He shifted beneath her. "Not that I'm complaining, because this is really nice. But if you want to keep sleeping, you'd better scoot over to your side of the bed."

She shifted her raised knee a bit and her eyebrow rose when it brushed against an increasingly hard ridge. "Again?"

"What can I say? You feel damn good."

Giving in to the inevitable, she opened her eyes. Seeing him lying on the pillow next to her, with his dark hair tumbling in his gleaming eyes, a shadow of morning beard on his strong jaw and a faint smile playing on his firm lips, made waking up worth the effort. "Anyone ever tell you that you're a gorgeous man?"

It wasn't often that she was able to fluster him, and it always amused her when she did. He blinked a few times, cleared his throat as if trying to decide how to respond to that, then grimaced lightly. "Uh, no. But thanks, I guess?"

She laughed and lifted her head to kiss his rough chin. "You're just so pretty."

"Yeah, okay. That's enough."

She touched the tip of her tongue to the corner of his mouth. "Bee-you-tee-ful."

Laughing now, he moved swiftly to flip her beneath him, looming over her. "You're just trying to get into trouble this morning, aren't you?"

She blinked innocently. "By telling you how handsome you are?"

He nipped her lower lip. "By trying to embarrass me."

Slipping a hand into the back of his hair, she drew his mouth down to hers and spoke against it. "I like teasing you," she admitted.

He kissed her lingeringly before murmuring, "Yeah, I got that."

"Besides," she added, sliding her arms around his bare shoulders, "it was all completely true."

He growled and took her mouth again, effectively silencing her.

It was some time later before they finally, regretfully, left the bed. Logan had confessed that he'd have been quite content to stay there all day, but he needed a shower and a shave. And food, he'd added, causing her to tease him again about his healthy appetites.

He shaved while she showered, then she dried her hair and put on a little makeup when he took his turn in the shower. They shared both bed and bath very naturally considering that this was the first weekend they'd spent together, she mused, putting away her mascara. She couldn't help remembering that moment last night when she'd worried that they were getting a little too comfortable together. She wasn't quite ready for the electricity between them to fizzle, as it always did with time, at least in her experience and observation. Maybe she'd be ready to let it go soon, but she wanted to hold on to it for just a little longer.

Seeing him emerge from the bathroom wearing only a pair of jeans, his hair damp and his chest gleaming from the hot shower, she swallowed hard.

Okay, so maybe the magic was still there for now. She could still appreciate the jolt she felt when she saw him like this. To be honest, she couldn't imagine ever *not* responding to seeing him like this.

He tugged a black T-shirt over his head. "So— museums, huh?"

Looking out the glass door, she saw that the rain had stopped and the clouds were lightening from charcoal to pale gray. The weather app on her phone informed her that the rain had stopped for the day, with partly cloudy skies and sixty-degree temperatures predicted for the afternoon. She was glad their last day in Seattle would be nice, weatherwise. She smiled as she reached for her bag and jacket. "No schedules today. Let's just go out and have a good time."

"Sounds good to me." He strapped on his watch, slid his wallet into his back pocket and shrugged into his own jacket. "But would you mind very much if we start with breakfast?"

She laughed. "Okay, we'll do that first. And I'll try not to run into anyone who recognizes me today."

Logan opened the door and motioned her out ahead of him. "That was unexpected."

"To say the least." She shook her head as they walked toward the elevator. "We come 2,700 miles to have a little time to ourselves, thinking there's no risk of being seen by anyone we know, and I hear my name in a club. Who'd have thought it?"

He chuckled and punched the call button. "It's not like we're fugitives hiding out from the law. I mean, even running into someone from back home who knows both of us wouldn't be the worst thing that could happen. It would be majorly weird, but hardly tragic."

"Don't even joke about that," she said, stepping into the elevator. "At least Isabella didn't know who you are, and because I very rudely didn't bother to introduce you, she doesn't have a name to share even if she should mention to any mutual acquaintances that she ran into me here. Not that she will, probably. Bella's kind of a ditz."

Leaning against the wall of the elevator, Logan studied her with a quirked eyebrow. "I wasn't really joking. About it not being the worst thing that could happen, I mean."

Maybe he was trying to reassure her that he wasn't upset that she'd been recognized. She doubted very much that he was implying that they should date openly back at home. Though she didn't want to analyze it right now, she found herself fighting near-panic at the very idea of making their relationship public. It would make it all seem so much more...complicated. Because she didn't want to spoil their last day here, she pushed the nerves away, deciding to focus only on the here and now. "What do you want for breakfast?"

"Food." He stood back and let her precede him out of the elevator into the hotel lobby.

Laughing softly, she headed for the exit doors with Logan close behind her.

"What a beautiful neighborhood."

Later that afternoon, Alexis turned in a slow circle to take in the scenery of Green Lake Park and the surrounding area. Obviously a popular place for locals, the almost-three-mile path around the glittering lake was crowded even on this cool, cloudy Saturday afternoon with walkers, runners, bikers, skateboarders, dog walkers, baby strollers. The paved path was divided into "wheels" and "feet" lanes, while a somewhat longer, higher trail seemed to attract more serious runners and power walkers. Teenagers sat on grassy hills, gossiping and listening to music, while birds and squirrels were active in the hundreds of trees that made up the natural park. Ducks and geese floated across the water and Alexis was pretty sure she spotted a bald eagle on the other side of the lake.

"If I were to move to Seattle, I think I'd want to live right there," she said, smiling as she pointed to a pretty Craftsman-style house sitting on a hill overlooking the park. "I'd walk around the lake every day, rain or shine, just to watch the wildlife and the parade of people."

His hands in his pockets, Logan studied her with a slight frown. "You thinking about moving?"

"No, I love Virginia. I just always like to imagine what it would be like to live in various places I visit."

He followed her gaze to the rows of houses lining the busy streets circling the park. "I've only lived in Tennessee and Virginia. I guess I haven't had what you'd call an exciting life. It's been a good one, though."

A young woman trying to control a barely leash-trained dog staggered toward them, both hands on the leash as her pet bounded over to them. Little more than an oversize puppy, the yellow Labrador retriever wriggled and panted, eager to explore and play. Perhaps recognizing a dog lover, he sniffed Logan's hand, his whole backside wagging in greeting. Logan laughed and rubbed the dog's ears. "Well, hey, there."

"I'm sorry," the young woman said. "He's still learning leash etiquette."

"No problem," Logan assured her. "Nice dog."

"Thanks. I just got him a few weeks ago. He's a handful."

The dog had already moved to Alexis, who petted him a couple of times before his owner dragged him away, somewhat futilely ordering him to "heel."

"This really is a doggy town," Alexis commented, counting at least half a dozen from where they stood. "You think any cat people live in Seattle?"

Logan shrugged. "Probably. Just not many people walk their cats."

As if to prove him wrong, an older man in jogging clothes and serious walking shoes strode briskly past them, accompanied by a black-and-white cat trotting beside him in a harness leash.

Alexis and Logan shared a look, then broke out laughing. She loved laughing with him.

They had just decided to leave the park and walk across the street for coffee when a frightened cry caught their attention. "Charlotte, stop! Come back right now!"

Alexis turned to see a streak of blue dash past her, headed straight for the water. Before she could even process what she'd seen, Logan was in motion. Throwing himself forward, he scooped the shrieking toddler into his arms just as she appeared ready to throw herself into the lake. Logan stumbled a bit and for a moment, Alexis was certain he was going in, as well.

He steadied himself almost immediately, and she re-leased the breath she'd caught.

The little girl squirmed and kicked in Logan's firm grip. "Wanna swim!" she bellowed. "Down!"

A woman in trendy running clothes and neon-pink athletic shoes rushed toward them, waving her hands frantically. "Ohmygosh, thank you so much! She just leaped out of her stroller and got away before I could stop her."

She motioned toward the expensive running stroller she'd abandoned on the path behind her. "I've just been having so much trouble keeping her in the stroller ever since she figured out how to unbuckle the strap. I looked away just a minute to chat with someone I recognized, and she took off."

"Wanna swim!" the unruly child insisted again, still struggling.

Holding her beneath her armpits, Logan held the toddler at arm's length toward her mother. "You should find a way to reinforce those buckles or to tie her in so she can't get out," he suggested with typi-cal bluntness.

The woman sighed gustily. "I know. It's just that she's so advanced for her age, and very curious. I'll explain to her that she can't swim in this cold weather. I'm sure she'll understand when we've talked."

She took the child away from him and turned to walk away, while Charlotte continued to vociferously demand to be set free.

Alexis looked up at Logan with wide eyes. "You saved that little girl's life!"

Looking embarrassed by the hyperbole, he mo-tioned briefly toward the spectators who'd gawked at them during the incident but now turned and returned to their walking, jogging, biking or skating.

"I doubt that I actually saved her life. She'd have been wet but someone still would have gotten to her."

"I thought what you did was amazing," she assured him.

He chuckled with little humor. "Now I really need that coffee."

"I'll buy."

She noticed as they headed for the closest coffee shop that he was limping somewhat more noticeably than usual. She waited until they were seated with their coffees—black for him, a flavored latte for her—before asking, "Did you hurt your leg when you jumped for the little girl?"

He dropped his hand quickly, as if he hadn't been aware he'd been massaging his left knee. "Nah. Twisted it a little. It's okay."

"You said you broke it playing sports?"

He took a long, careful sip of his coffee and she got the distinct impression that he was delaying his answer. "Yeah. Long time ago." He changed the subject quickly, now sounding a little weary from their day of walking and sightseeing, but still game to keep her entertained. "So, what else do you want to do on our last day in Seattle?"

Cradling her coffee cup in her hands, she smiled at him. "I would like to have another nice dinner, and then I'd like to go back to our room and sit on our balcony with a bottle of good wine and admire the lights on the water. After that—well, I'm sure we'll think of something to do."

She could almost see the relief in his eyes. "Have I ever mentioned that I like the way your mind works?"

"And I thought you just wanted my body."

His lips curved upward. "That, too."

Pleased that she'd made him smile again, she finished her latte quickly.

"Are you sure all those gift shop purchases are going to fit in your bags?" Logan teased Sunday morning, watching as Alexis carefully tucked two large packages of MarketSpice cinnamon-orange tea bags in the suitcase she would check at the gate. She'd tasted the tea at Pike Place Market and had been unable to resist taking some home with her. She figured that every time she drank a cup of the strong, fragrant brew, she would be mentally transported back to these lovely days with Logan.

"I didn't buy that much," she said, folding a beautiful scarf she'd found downtown around a pretty coffee mug she'd bought at the art museum. The mug was wrapped in Bubble Wrap and sealed in a cardboard box, but she wanted it to have plenty of protection. The little ceramic Space Needle replica fit nicely into a shoe, which she figured would keep it safe. She was wearing the dangling earrings she'd bought from an artist in a booth at the market, so she didn't have to bother packing them.

She looked up to find Logan grinning at her, and she wrinkled her nose. "Okay, I'm a sucker for souvenirs. You don't want to take anything home as a memento of your visit here?"

He tapped his temple with one finger. "I've got it all stored up here. Won't forget a minute of it."

She stifled a sigh. It really had been a magical weekend. Fun days, and delicious nights. She wouldn't forget any of it, either—with or without the souvenirs.

He glanced at his watch. "Have you got everything? It's almost time to head downstairs."

"You're sure you want to go to the airport at the same time I do? You'll be sitting there more than three hours until your flight leaves." His plane was scheduled to leave nearly two hours after hers, but he'd said he might as well head to the airport at the same time she did. He had no interest in hanging around downtown by himself for a couple hours.

"I'll be fine. I've got a paperback spy novel in my carry-on. I'm only about a third of the way in, but it's pretty good so far."

She supposed she didn't have to worry about Logan keeping himself entertained. He was one of the most self-sufficient people she knew.

She took a long look around the room, purportedly to make sure she had everything, but really to silently say goodbye. Drawing a deep breath, she turned back to Logan then. "Okay, I'm ready."

Sea-Tac Airport wasn't very crowded this early on a Sunday, so they made it through security easily enough. Knowing there would be time to kill, they'd waited to have breakfast at the airport. They didn't talk about anything of particular import as they munched on Dungeness crab breakfast sandwiches washed down with coffee, but she suspected the return to Virginia weighed as heavily on his mind as it did on hers. She didn't deny that her own feelings were mixed. She looked forward to getting back to her home, her cat and her work, but she'd had fun here with Logan. Seattle was an interesting city and she'd like to explore more of it sometime. She wouldn't mind doing so with him.

Having eaten, they wandered into a gift shop that advertised goods made in Washington and she couldn't resist buying another pretty scarf in a mix of bright spring colors. She tucked it into her carry-on bag, pretending to ignore Logan's broad grin. And then she bought a bottle of water to carry onto the plane with her in case she got thirsty on the long flight. Her tablet computer was tucked into her bag with several books loaded on it. She would keep her mind busy during the journey, the better to not spend the time worrying about whether this weekend had changed things too greatly between her and Logan.

"I'm really not a shopaholic," she informed him loftily, heading for her gate. "I don't buy much at home. I just really like gift shops."

"Wow, I never would have figured that out."

She laughed and punched his arm. Rubbing it, he reminded her that the airport was filled with security cameras and she wouldn't want to be charged with assault and battery. He wrapped the same arm casually around her shoulders as they looked for an empty bench at her gate, and she leaned companionably into him. She couldn't help thinking that this was probably the last time in the foreseeable future that they'd be so comfortably familiar in a public place, which gave her a funny feeling in her stomach. Maybe the crab sandwich had been a little too rich on an empty stomach.

"So, busy week ahead at home?" he asked her.

"Very. A lot of catch-up stuff, a couple of events,

some big weddings coming up. One at the inn in a couple weeks."

She knew he didn't choose to know about upcoming events until it was time for him to be involved. "Simple and sweet?"

She smiled faintly. "Well, not too complicated. Another spring theme, plenty of pastels. It will take place just after sunset, and they want lots of fairy lights and candles, but that's about the extent of the decorations they've requested. The dance and dinner afterward will be held elsewhere."

He nodded. "We'll take care of them."

She reached out to cover his hand with hers. "I know you will."

He squeezed her fingers, then kept his hand wrapped around hers. They sat rather quietly until the gate attendant announced boarding for Alexis's flight. Logan stood with her, making sure she had her tote bag and carry-on, her boarding pass in hand. "Have a safe flight," he said. "I'll see you back home in a few days."

She nodded, smiling despite the lump in her throat. "You travel safely, too. I hope you don't have any delays."

He cupped a hand behind her head and leaned down to kiss her lingeringly. One last public display? Or maybe a prelude to an end? Either way, it left her feeling a little sad. "See you when I see you," she murmured.

He nodded and turned away, presumably to head to his own gate. With a hard swallow, she boarded her plane.

Chapter Nine

"Logan, that's not right. We don't want any blue lights, only pink and yellow and green."

With a scowl, he looked down from the tall ladder propped against the gazebo. "Are you kidding me?"

Hands on her hips, Alexis gazed back up at him. "Pink, yellow and green," she repeated. "No blue."

"She's right, Logan," Kinley seconded from beside her. "It's in the orders."

He sighed heavily and started down the ladder.

Around them, frantic preparations were taking place for the wedding that would start in only a couple of hours. Back at work part-time after his appendectomy, but still not cleared to do any heavy lifting, young Zach helped the florist's employees set up a half dozen freestanding white wrought-iron candelabra, each holding six tall tapers in the chosen pastels.

Curtis and his brother-in-law were setting out spring flowers in big pots also wound with strings of fairy lights. The folding white chairs had already been set out in rows facing the gazebo. The aisle chair in each row would be decorated with a nosegay of ribbon and flowers and battery-powered fairy lights to be turned on just before the first guests were due to arrive. Once the sun set, the grounds would be aglow with tiny pastel lights and candle flames in addition to the soft path lighting and upward-pointing fountain lights that were always on in the gardens. It would be just the romantic scene the bride had requested.

Logan looked into the big box he'd brought down with him from the ladder shelf. "Why are there strings of blue lights in the box that was delivered to me?"

"Obviously an error," his sister retorted. "Please tell me the other colors are in there."

He dug through the box. "Yeah. Pink, yellow, green and blue."

"Don't use the blue," his sister ordered.

"Yeah, I got that," he grumbled, frowning up at the garland that he'd already wound with strings of pink and blue lights before Alexis and Kinley had checked on the progress of the decorations. "I'll have to take out the blue strand and put in the others. What's wrong with blue, anyway?"

"It just doesn't match her theme," Alexis replied.

He gave her a look, but shrugged. "Fine. I'll fix it. Anything else?"

She shook her head. "Everything's looking very nice. Thank you, Lo—"

Her words were cut off when she was bumped abruptly from behind. She looked around and then down to find Ninja sitting at her feet, his tail wagging on the grass. He grinned up at her around a white rose held carefully between his teeth, and then he reached out and laid the flower at her feet.

"Ninja!" Kinley groaned loudly and snatched up the flower. "Where did you get this? I swear, if you've ruined one of the baskets…"

"Zach!" Even as he yelled the name, Logan took hold of his dog's collar. "Did you leave the padlock off the gate to my yard when you got that push broom from the storage shed?"

Zach grimaced. "Yeah, maybe," he confessed. "But I made sure the gate was latched."

Logan blew out a hard breath of exasperation. "You know he can open the latch."

"I found the basket where he got the rose," one of the florist employees called from the other side of the gravel aisle path. "It's fine, he took it right off the outside."

Kinley carried the undamaged bloom in that direction.

Zach stepped forward to reach for the dog's collar. "I'll take him back. And I'll put the padlock on this time."

"Don't fuss at him, he didn't cause any harm," Alexis said, bending to pet the dog, who was wagging a bit more tentatively now. "Thank you for the gift," she whispered in his ear, "but you'd better be good for the rest of the day."

He nuzzled her face, knocking her glasses askew, his low, affectionate rumble vibrating in his broad chest. Giving him one last pat, she straightened and moved aside so Zach could lead Ninja away.

"You're still spoiling him," Logan accused in a tone low enough that only Alexis could hear.

She flashed a smile at him. "Sorry, I can't help it. He's such a sweetie."

Their gazes held for a moment until Kinley returned to them. "Okay, no damage done," she reported. She looked quizzically at Alexis. "That mutt sure does like you."

Alexis smiled brightly. "He knows I like him, too. I was just telling Logan that his pet is a sweetie."

"His pet is a scoundrel."

Laughing, Alexis nodded. "Maybe that's what I like about him."

Logan turned on one boot heel toward his ladder. "I've got to take the blue lights out of this garland and put in the yellow and green. Let me know if there's anything else, but give me time to take care of it if there is."

Alexis could have stood there a while longer, just watching him on the ladder. It was a pleasantly moderate Saturday afternoon in mid-April, so he wasn't wearing a jacket, just jeans and boots and a navy T-shirt that bared his strong arms and molded to his broad back and chest and shoulders. She could pretend to be simply monitoring his work, but that would just annoy him, and she had too many other things to do before the guests began to arrive. She made herself turn away.

"I'm glad we caught that mistake," Kinley said with a shake of her head. "It's not that the pale blue would look so bad with the other colors, but that isn't what the bride wants."

Alexis shrugged. "Considering how late we're running with everything else today, if that's the worst problem we encounter, we're lucky." There had been a series of minor glitches that day, beginning with an unexpected April shower that morning that had delayed setup of some of the decorations, but fortunately had passed quickly.

Alexis always fretted when brides were determined to hold outdoor weddings in these unpredictable spring months, but all she could do when they insisted was to make as many contingency plans as possible and try to satisfy her clients' wishes. Though she'd been busy with several indoor affairs, this was the first outdoor event she'd supervised since she'd returned from Seattle two weeks ago tomorrow. Thank goodness. April had brought several spring storms with it, twice bordering on severe weather that would have made outdoor events impossible. At least this afternoon had turned out nice once the early shower passed.

Kinley let out a little sigh. "It's been a crazy few weeks around here. Seems like we've been putting out one fire after another, but maybe it'll ease up a little when the weather stabilizes. Let's hope that's soon. Those storms last week had Logan pacing the floor for fear we'd lose shingles or trees."

Alexis didn't say, of course, that she knew that already. She and Logan had been too busy to get together since they'd returned, but they'd spoken several times by phone. She knew he was ready for spring storms to pass into the more typically stable summer weather.

To be perfectly honest, she was the one who'd kept them from getting together. Yes, he'd been busy, too, especially with the storms and the resulting cleanup, and she had been heavily scheduled for both day-time and evening appointments during the past two weeks, but probably there'd have been time to spend a couple hours together if she'd tried hard enough. Instead, she'd found herself making excuses, putting him off with assurances that they would get together soon. Not because she hadn't wanted to see him, but because she'd wanted it a little too much. Paradoxically, the more she'd missed him, the more concerned she'd been about seeing him again.

She had practically ached for him during those first days after she'd returned from Seattle. She'd found herself reaching out in the night to touch him, or waking with the expectation of seeing his face on the pillow next to hers. She shouldn't have gotten that accustomed to sleeping with him after only three nights, should she? She had decided that perhaps a little distance between them would help them get back into their previous routine, which had worked so well before. After all, it was always an adjustment to get back to real life after a particularly nice vacation.

Logan hadn't questioned her excuses that she'd been too busy to get together, especially since he, too, had been kept on the run, but she'd sensed his growing impatience. Maybe it was time to spend a couple hours together again, just to make sure nothing had changed. Or maybe to acknowledge that too much had changed to continue as they had before.

"Anyway," Kinley went on, oblivious to Alexis's inner turmoil, "with everything that's been going on, we still haven't a chance to get together for lunch. Maybe sometime next week?"

"I'd like that," Alexis replied, though she couldn't help but be aware of the pitfalls of spending time with Logan's sister.

"Curtis!" Logan called from behind them. "These lights aren't getting any juice. Check the plugs."

Alexis grimaced. She didn't even want to know if there were new problems.

Kinley patted her arm. "Logan will take care of it."

"Yes, I'm sure he will."

"I know we're a little behind because of the rain this morning, but don't worry, we'll be ready."

Alexis glanced over her shoulder, watching in relief as the tiny pastel lights wound into the garland over the gazebo opening suddenly came on. Whatever Curtis had done, it had worked. The florist employees were busily attaching the nosegays to the aisle chairs now, and a few members of the wedding party who'd stayed at the inn last night were chattering up on the deck, their anticipation building. She was accustomed to the chaos that preceded even the most serene ceremony, so she wasn't overly concerned, though she didn't like cutting it this close. "It's looking great."

Seeing her looking his way, Logan gave her a quick thumbs-up, then went back to work.

"He's been in a little better mood since Bonnie made him take a vacation," Kinley commented, following the brief exchange. "He's being very mysterious about where he went—we think he just enjoys making us crazy that way—but Bonnie thinks maybe he went to Las Vegas."

"Oh? What makes her think that?"

"He went there once with some friends a few years

ago for a bachelor party, and he had a great time. He's always said he wanted to go back sometime."

He'd never mentioned Las Vegas to her, Alexis mused. She wouldn't have thought the deliberately, outrageously tacky tourist town would appeal to him. Despite how intimate they'd been, he could still manage to surprise her.

"Curtis!" Logan bellowed from behind them.

Kinley placed a hand on Alexis's arm and kept walking. "Of course, he is still Logan. The mellow mood he was in when he came back from vacation has been sort of wearing off."

Alexis cleared her throat and tried to think what to say. Fortunately, she didn't have to come up with anything because her phone rang and she had to attend to her business. Only later did it occur to her that Kinley hadn't revealed her own guess as to where Logan had spent his vacation.

Darkness was falling and the wedding party had arrived when Logan checked the grounds one last time. From where he stood by the fountain, he could see the whole wedding setting. The gazebo looked good, rising proudly from the gardens and illuminated by meticulously placed lights. The musicians and their instruments were in place on the gazebo floor, just starting the first romantic number. The garland draped over the arched opening where the officiant, bride and groom would stand glowed softly with pastel pink, yellow and green—no blue—fairy lights. More lights twinkled among flowers and ribbons on the chairs at the ends of rows, in baskets and pots of flowers lining the path. Candles were being lit as he watched, and the ushers were taking positions to escort early-arriving guests to their seats. He glanced at his watch, noting that the wedding was supposed to start in exactly twenty minutes. There was no more he could do until it was over and he would start taking down what he'd spent all afternoon putting in place.

Concealed in the shadows outside the glow of lights and candles, he looked for Alexis, spotting her bustling around the outside of the dressing rooms, no doubt hurrying the bride and her attendants along. She was focused intently on her responsibilities as director of this production, and he knew without doubt that nothing was more important to her at the moment than making her clients happy. In intriguing contrast to the woman who'd loved playing tourist and buying cheap souvenirs in Seattle, she was all business now, even her smiles more polished and purposeful.

Damn, but he wished he could whisk her away right now to someplace they could be completely alone, just the two of them and a bed. Had it really been only two weeks since they'd been in a bed together? It felt like more.

"Hello."

He looked around to nod at the tuxedo-clad man who'd greeted him from the other side of the fountain. When the man stepped into the light, Logan recognized him from an earlier meeting. "Aren't you supposed to be getting married?"

The groom, Tate Webber, shrugged. "I've got a few minutes before I have to be in place. Thought I'd take a little walk first."

Logan eyed him suspiciously. "Not getting cold feet, are you?"

He wouldn't even be the first client who tried to back out of the wedding literally at the last minute; they'd had a bride who'd locked herself in a bathroom a year ago after a fight with her mother and had tearfully declared that her wedding was off. Kinley had handled the crisis, calming down the hysterical bride and convincing her she did want to go through with it. Kinley had sworn later that she hadn't strong-armed the bride; had she truly wanted to call off the ceremony, Kinley would have taken care of that, too. He wondered if he was going to have to summon Kinley now.

But the groom-to-be shook his head with a weak smile. "No. I want to marry Becca. Just a little stage fright, I guess. I'm not comfortable standing up and talking in front of people."

Glancing at the chairs slowly filling in front of the gazebo, Logan said, "Doesn't look like you invited hundreds of guests."

"No. We decided on a smallish wedding, just close friends and relatives."

"Then it's no big deal, right? Just look at your bride and forget about everyone else."

"Yeah, I'll do that. The place looks really nice, by the way. Becca wanted it to look like a fairyland, and I guess that's what you gave her with all those candles and little lights."

"Thanks, but I just put the stuff where I was told to. Al— Er, your wedding planner is the one who came up with all the plans for decorations."

"Yeah, she's pretty good, huh? I didn't know why we needed a planner at all. I told Becca I thought we could put it all together ourselves, since we didn't want anything too elaborate. But I've got to admit Alexis made everything a lot easier for us. She took care of the flowers and the musicians and photographers and stuff. She helped everyone find the right clothes and accommodations and she negotiated some pretty good prices for us on stuff. I'm real glad we decided to work with her."

"She's worked several events here. Everyone seems to leave satisfied afterward."

It was the most he would allow himself to praise her, but he'd made his point. Alexis was good at her job, despite the occasional silly request, which he supposed he should blame more on her clients than on her.

"Man, I can't believe this day is finally here," Tate said, sounding a little dazed. "We were supposed to get married two years ago, but I was in a bad car accident right after we got engaged, before we even had a chance to set a date."

Logan wasn't quite sure what to say. "I hadn't heard that. You're okay now, I guess?"

The groom smiled crookedly and only then did Logan notice that one side of the guy's face didn't move quite the same as the other. "I had what they call a TBI—a traumatic brain injury. Becca stood by me every minute, even when it looked bad. I had to learn to walk and talk and stuff again. Kind of why I'm still a bit shaky talking in front of people."

"You're talking fine to me," Logan pointed out, impressed by how far the slightly younger guy had come.

"I still stammer a little when I get nervous, but it'll be okay. Just as long as we make it legal. The whole time I was working to get better, this was my goal, to make Becca my wife." Unashamedly emotional, the guy swiped at his eyes with the back of one hand. "Sorry. Still struggle with a little lability."

Logan shrugged, typically uncomfortable with the display of sentiment but thinking no less of the guy for showing it. "You're not the only groom who's gotten emotional before the big event."

Tate's pocket buzzed and he pulled out a phone and checked the screen. "I'm being summoned. Thanks again for putting up all those little pink and yellow lights for Becca. It's just what she likes."

Nodding, Logan held out a hand. "Congratulations. And good luck."

Tate shook his hand with a broad grin that was no less contagious because of the asymmetry. "Thanks. I figure I've been given a second chance. I'm not going to mess it up."

A second chance. Logan stood for several long minutes without moving after the groom hurried off, replaying those words in his mind. He turned away as the ceremony began, uncharacteristically aware of his slight limp when he moved toward his cottage.

Alexis sometimes thought her cat could read her mind, which was a rather spooky feeling. Fiona seemed to know Sunday afternoon that Logan was expected, and that Alexis had invited him to bring Ninja, if he wanted. The cat wandered restlessly through the house, meowing and looking at the door as if impatient for it to open, even though she was an indoor-only cat who never wanted out. As restless as the cat, Alexis busied herself in the kitchen making brownies to offer Logan when he arrived. She had just taken them out of the oven when the doorbell chimed. Fiona scrabbled on the tile kitchen floor, then dashed toward the living room.

Ninja greeted Alexis with a nuzzle and a cheery rumble, then trotted off to play with Fiona, who was already winding around him and rubbing her head against him. The little gray cat was dwarfed by the dog, but it was obvious that she considered them equals and friends.

Alexis looked at Logan with a laugh. "That could be the oddest couple ever."

"They are definitely unique," he agreed, closing the door behind him. "The house smells good."

"I made brownies. And coffee. Want some?"

He gazed down at her with a gleam in his hazel eyes. "Maybe later."

Okay, so things felt a bit more normal now. He wasn't here to make small talk or share confidences or any of those other little niceties that would make them feel like an established couple. It was just as it had always been before their anomalous trip to Seattle had left her worried about changing expectations—though she wasn't sure if she'd been more concerned about his or her own. She assured herself she was quite relieved, actually, that he didn't want to change anything.

She stepped into his arms and lifted her face to him. "I think Fiona and Ninja would like to be alone for a while."

"Do you?"

"Absolutely."

"Then by all means."

She sputtered in surprise and laughter when he

swept her into his arms and carried her toward the bedroom.

He was already hard and ready by the time he tumbled her onto the bed, his hands busily tugging at her shirt and jeans.

"Wow," she said when she emerged from the shirt he swept over her head, dislodging her glasses along with it. She set them quickly aside.

Logan's grin could definitely be described as roguish. "It's been a very long time."

She could have replied that two weeks wasn't such a long time. That they'd gone longer than that in the past without seeing each other. But the thing was, these past two weeks had seemed very long to her, too. And she was just as eager to get him out of his clothes.

As always, passion flared quickly between them when they finally lay skin to skin. Still, Logan slowed his movements, taking time to savor, appreciate, pleasure. He was always a generous lover, but there seemed to be a new element to his caresses tonight. A tenderness that took her off guard, that brought a hard lump to her throat even as his clever fingers drove her to the point of dazed incoherence.

She had to make a concerted effort to regain some control, to push against his shoulders and roll him onto his back to grant her lips access to his throat, his chest and lower. She ran her hands over him, tracing muscle and bone, planes and angles, sleek skin and scars. Loving every inch of him she touched.

Her hands froze as the word echoed discordantly in her mind. Loving? No. She appreciated him. She was wildly attracted to him. She liked him very much.

But that was all there was to it. All she would allow it to be.

Taking advantage of her sudden stillness, he rolled her beneath him, his mouth seeking hers, his tongue plunging to tangle with hers. She pushed semantics aside, choosing instead to focus solely on the physical.

He cupped her face between his hands as he pushed into her. She felt the tremors running through his fingers, the rigidity of the muscles beneath her palms, both signs of the fierce control he exerted. She wrapped herself around him, urging him on, moving her mouth more feverishly against his until his restraint broke and he swept them both into madness.

She had no idea how much time passed before she could think clearly again, before her heart returned to a somewhat regular rhythm. Logan was still breathing a little heavily, but his eyes were open when she turned onto her right side to look at him. His mouth curved in a satisfied smile. She adjusted her pillow beneath her right cheek to more comfortably study him.

"So it really was a long two weeks, hmm?" she asked, her voice husky.

He put his right arm behind his head, sprawling unself-consciously nude against her tumbled sheets, his left leg bent up at the knee next to her. "You have no idea."

Laughing softly, she said, "And then I came along with the blue-light kerfuffle to top off your day."

He chuckled. "The blue-light kerfuffle?"

"Followed by the white-rose episode. Although that was more Ninja's fault than mine."

"Dumb dog," he said indulgently.

"Oh, he's far from dumb. In fact, he seems a little

too intent on making it clear that he knows me better than we've let on."

Logan shrugged. "It's not like he can talk."

She glanced toward the doorway. "I wouldn't be particularly surprised if he could."

He gave an exaggerated sigh and shook his head. "He's a dog."

"Yes. A very strange and special dog, like my strange and special cat."

He laughed softly.

She ran her hand affectionately along his raised leg, over hair and tendon and scars. "Ready for brownies and coffee now?"

There was a short silence before he replied, and for some reason she didn't think he was considering the merits of dessert. But whatever had distracted him, he shook it off and said, "Yeah, that sounds good. Where'd my pants land?"

Giggling, she reached for her robe.

Chapter Ten

Fully dressed, Logan joined her in the kitchen a short time later. He glanced at their pets, who were companionably enjoying treats in one corner of the kitchen, then took a seat at the table. "Spoiling my dog again?"

She smiled and set a plate of brownies and a cup of coffee in front of him. "He thinks I'm spoiling you."

"So you have been talking to him?"

"I can read his expressions," she retorted, serving herself a brownie and sinking into a chair.

"Now you sound like Bonnie." He sipped his coffee, then put down his cup, his expression suddenly serious.

She cocked her head, sensing that there was something he wanted to say. "What?"

"When we were in bed a few minutes ago—you brushed the scars on my leg with your hand."

"Yes—I'm sorry, does that bother you?"

He shook his head. "Doesn't bother me. Some other people have been turned off by them, though."

"Seriously? They don't bother me, other than how I hate thinking of the pain you must have felt when you got them."

"You've never asked questions about them."

"I never thought you wanted to talk about it," she said with a light shrug, wondering where this was going. "You told me it was a sports injury from college, and I figured that was all I needed to know."

"It started with an injury the day after I turned twenty-one," he confirmed. "I broke my leg playing rugby. It was when they were treating the break that the doctors discovered a tumor."

She dropped the brownie she'd just picked up. "A tumor? You mean...cancer?"

He nodded, his eyes dark with memories. "It was on the bone. I had surgery to remove the tumor, another operation later to make some repairs, but at least I didn't have to lose the leg. I had to have chemotherapy—which meant I lost my hair for a while and lost a ridiculous amount of weight."

Wide-eyed, she looked at his thick, dark hair, at the muscles that strained against his T-shirt. No wonder he was so into health and fitness now. "I...had no idea" was all she could think of to say.

"As you guessed, I don't much like to talk about it. My sisters don't mention it because they know I'd rather they didn't. It's not like it's a state secret, but it was a part of my life I prefer not to dwell on."

"I can understand that." It must have been a horrible time—for him, for his sisters, for his mother and great-uncle and others who had loved him. "Were you... Was your life in danger?"

"Fortunately it was caught very early because of the sports injury. The cancer hadn't yet spread, which would have made survival less likely. Worst part was an infection that set in after the second operation. I was pretty sick for a while, but obviously I recovered. I'm completely well now, just have to check in with a doctor once a year, but all my reports are clean. I've passed the ten-year survival mark, which is a big deal. The limp will be with me for life, but considering the alternatives, that's a fairly minor annoyance."

"No kidding." She understood a little better why he didn't like talking about the past. But why was he telling her all of this now?

"You asked about my leg once in Seattle," he said as if he'd sensed her question. "I put you off then, because I didn't want to talk about it in a coffee shop. But I can understand why you'd be curious about the scars, so I figured now was as good a time as any to tell you about it."

"Does it still hurt you?"

He shook his head. "Gets a little sore every once in a while when I overuse it, and sometimes I swear I can tell when it's going to rain, but it doesn't hold me back from what I want to do."

"I always just accepted you'd messed up the leg in a sports accident. Considering the scars and the limp, I assumed it was a really bad break and I figured you'd been though a lot of pain with it. I had no idea you're a cancer survivor."

He shrugged and picked up his brownie, avoiding

her searching eyes. "Injury, cancer. Doesn't change who I am."

She couldn't help wondering how much it changed who he had been before. Had he emerged from the ordeal with inner scars as well as outer ones? Had he always been somewhat solitary, blunt-spoken and occasionally cranky, or had the illness reinforced that side of him? Now that she'd learned a little more about him, she found herself even more curious than she'd been before.

"You were so young."

"The type of cancer I had is most common in young males. Actually, I was on the upper end of the typical age range."

"I know your family must have been a great source of support for you during that time."

"Of course. My mom was there every step of the way. Kinley was in college herself, and she got into the habit of studying in my room to keep me company when I was too weak to get up. Bonnie was a senior in high school. She took over most of the housework and cooking so Mom could keep her job and still take care of me. No surprise, Bonnie's always been happy to cook and clean and do domestic-type things."

No wonder he and his sisters were so close now—not just because they were the only family they had left, but because they knew how lucky they were to still have each other. "And your dad?" she asked tentatively, knowing she was stepping onto shaky ground. "Was he there for you?"

"Financially, yes," he said after a hesitation. "He made sure I didn't lack for anything, that Mom stayed afloat with the bills. I think he pretty much sent us everything he made for a couple of years, holding back just enough to let him eat and have a roof of sorts over his head. He came to see me a couple times. He was living in South America then, so it wasn't such a long commute. But each time, he said he couldn't stay long because he thought it was more important to get back to work and provide income than to sit by my bedside."

He drew a breath and pushed a hand through his hair. "Truth was, he's the type who doesn't deal well with illness. During that year, I learned it's not such an uncommon trait."

"Your friends?"

"Friends. Fiancée. They were young, active, couldn't deal with it. A few buddies hung in there with me. Some of them are still good friends today, though we live in different areas. I've got some friends here. A couple of guys I met during my summers here when I was growing up, some I've met through them and in pickup sports at the park. As you know, I don't have a lot of spare time to hang out, but I try to meet up with some of them at least once a month or so. None of them know about the cancer, so they don't treat me any different than they do any of the other guys. I don't mention it because the reactions are so often weird—people either treat me like I'm possibly contagious, or like some sort of damned hero just because I didn't die."

She tucked the word *fiancée* away to think about later. Actually maybe she'd think about all of this later, after she'd had time to process it. "You've made a good life for yourself now."

"I have. All in all, I'm a lucky guy."

She glanced at his dog, who was curled on a black-

and-white kitchen rug with her cat snoozing on top of him, and she couldn't help but smile faintly at the sight. "Ninja's a lucky guy, too, to have wandered into your yard."

Logan chuckled. He looked greatly relieved that she'd changed the subject so matter-of-factly. "Yeah. Ninja and I have got it good, don't we, pal?"

Without opening his eyes, the dog thumped his tail on the floor.

Logan wiped his mouth on a paper napkin and drained his coffee. "That was good, Alexis. Thanks."

Putting all heavy topics behind them, she stood to clear the table, winking at him when she said, "You're welcome. I know certain activities make you hungry."

He caught her around the waist before she'd even realized he'd risen from the chair. Spinning her into his arms, he planted a hard kiss on her lips, then raised his head with a wicked grin. "I'm always hungry around you. Just not necessarily for food."

She laughed, gave him a little nip on his chin, then slipped out of his arms. "You silver-tongued devil, you."

"Can't say I've been called that before."

She smiled over her shoulder as she set their plates in the sink. "Maybe I just bring out the glib side of you."

"Maybe you do." He looked at the clock and pulled his keys out of his pocket. "I'm going to take off now. I've got a meeting with a software client in town late Tuesday afternoon. Should be done by about six. If you're free that evening, how would you like if I bring a pizza and we stream a movie or something?"

"Tuesday?" She did a quick mental run-through of

her upcoming schedule, at the same time surprised that he'd asked. They didn't usually get together so often and he'd never suggested a quiet movie night. The word *domestic* hovered uncomfortably in her mind for a moment, but she told herself she was over-thinking. As he'd said, he was going to be in town, anyway. It made sense for him to come by for dinner.

"I'm free Tuesday evening," she said, thinking she'd have time for the paperwork she'd planned to do that evening after he left. Probably he wouldn't stay too late if he was coming over that early. "Pizza sounds good. Light on the tomato sauce."

"You got it." He kissed her, gave her a playful squeeze on the butt, then called his dog and let himself out of the house.

Alexis tightened the sash of her robe, then bent to pick up Fiona, snuggling the warm cat in her arms as she walked into the living room to lock up for the night.

Something had been different tonight. Logan had been different. Even before he'd surprised her by telling her about a part of his life he said few of his friends here even knew about, she'd sensed a slight change in him. The way he'd looked at her when he'd arrived. The way he'd swept her off her feet to carry her to the bedroom. Even the extra tenderness he'd displayed in their lovemaking. Though she couldn't quite define it, something had changed.

It must have happened during their vacation in Se-attle. After all, tonight had been the first time they'd been alone together since.

She supposed it was inevitable that those days and nights together had added a new dimension to their relationship. A new intimacy. They'd each learned things about the other during the trip. For example, she'd heard for the first time about the unscrupulous business partner he'd considered a friend. That betrayal had to have hurt him. Now she knew he'd survived even more blows than she'd realized. His father's abandonment. Surviving a terrible illness. Losing friends—and a woman he'd thought he loved enough to be engaged to her. Betrayed by his partner. Losing his mother. Losing his beloved great-uncle. No wonder he'd become so prickly. And yet...

She thought of the way he supported his sisters in anything they wanted. Grumbling at times, but always coming through for them. She wouldn't want to be the man who hurt either of them if their occasionally intimidating brother was around to champion them. She considered his gift of arranging garland and fairy lights to make a bride gasp with delight. His kindness toward animals—the bond he'd formed with a "quirky" stray, his patience with her attention-loving cat. His dry sense of humor. The way he made her feel beautiful and desirable and sexy without flowery words or studiedly amorous gestures.

Sudden panic gripped her, squeezing the breath out of her. She didn't want to think of him like this. Didn't want to admire him so much or understand him so well. It was supposed to be easy between them. Casual. Superficial. Sensible and realistic. That was all she wanted. All she could handle for now. She simply would not risk anything more.

It had hurt her badly enough when Harry had told her that he no longer wanted her as part of his life. That the passion had faded, the excitement was over, the feelings were gone. The same things her parents had said to each other years earlier. Things her brother had probably said to his two ex-wives. Even imagining hearing those words, or variations thereof, from Logan made her whole body tighten in dread.

Fiona squirmed and meowed, and Alexis realized she must have tightened her grip a bit too much. "Sorry," she murmured, setting the cat down and stroking her in apology. "I was just being silly."

She was, of course. Logan had made it clear from the start that he wasn't looking for permanence or romance. He'd given her no reason to make her believe he'd changed his mind, right? No promises, no potential grief.

So maybe he'd shared a little more of his past with her. They were friends. Friends talked. It didn't have to mean anything more than that.

They'd have pizza Tuesday night, she thought, heading for the bedroom with her chin up, her mouth set in a resolute line. Probably they'd have sex. And then he would leave, as he always did, and they'd turn their attentions to their individual busy schedules. After that, they'd stay in touch with occasional friendly phone calls, get together when they could— certainly not as often once the wedding season picked up. And when they mutually agreed the affair had run its course, they would end it as friendly associates, just the way they'd agreed from the start.

Feeling much better now, she got ready for bed, then climbed beneath the covers while Fiona curled up beside her. But it was the memory of being held against Logan's warm, bare chest that accompanied her into sleep.

* * *

The scents of melted cheese and steaming vegetables filled the cab of Logan's pickup as he parked in Alexis's driveway Tuesday evening. He juggled the box and the bottle of good red wine he'd brought as he climbed out of the truck and headed for her front door. He'd actually considered bringing flowers. He'd seen a display when he'd stopped for the wine and he'd found himself debating between roses and daisies before he'd stopped himself. He would buy her flowers sometime, but not tonight. She'd think he was up to something for sure if he showed up with dinner and wine *and* flowers.

She opened the door with a smile that was so bright it almost glittered. He wasn't entirely sure it reached her eyes, but she looked down at his hands before he could study them through her glasses. Maybe she was just tired. She'd said she would be putting in some hard hours this week.

"That smells delicious," she said, ushering him inside. "I'm really hungry. I had a salad for lunch and that was hours ago."

"Good. I'm starving, too, so let's eat while it's hot." He handed her the wine, which she studied approvingly before turning to get wineglasses.

Fiona walked a big circle around Logan, meowing and obviously looking for Ninja. When she conceded that her friend hadn't come, she made a show of turning her back on Logan and stalking away, tail in the air to express her displeasure.

He laughed. "Your cat makes her feelings known, doesn't she?"

"Very much so."

They talked about work during the meal, discussing the things they'd done since they'd parted Sunday night, chatting about upcoming obligations. Alexis had nothing scheduled at the inn for the next few weeks, though she had several events scheduled at other venues. She had a big wedding at a church on the coming Saturday evening and that, in addition to her usual meetings and duties, would keep her occupied for the rest of this week, she said. Logan told her he would stay occupied for the next few days with spring plantings in the gardens and numerous flower beds surrounding the inn, along with some routine maintenance chores.

When they'd eaten their fill, he helped her with cleanup and then they carried their wineglasses into the living room and sat side by side on the couch, though Alexis didn't immediately reach for the television remote. Proving she'd forgiven him, Fiona leaped onto his lap to head-butt his hand in a demand for strokes and scratches, which he obligingly provided.

"Did your software meeting go well?" Alexis asked.

"Yeah, he was satisfied with the report I'd prepared for him. I made several recommendations that will streamline his operation and let him spend less time on paperwork. He's been wasting a couple hours a week on redundant forms that could easily be consolidated in one program."

"Hmm. Maybe I should hire you to look at the programs Gretchen and I use for my business," she mused, obviously impressed. "Saving us a couple hours a week on record-keeping and ordering would be well worth the cost—assuming your services are affordable, of course," she teased.

"For you—very."

She frowned and shook her head, not exactly the response he'd expected though he probably should have. "I'd want to pay your usual rates, of course. I wasn't asking for favoritism. Remember, we agreed to keep our personal relationship totally separate from business."

"I remember," he said with a slight shake of his head. Heaven forbid he step on her professional pride, he thought in mild exasperation. "If you're serious, I'll look at your operation at my usual hourly consultation fee, less a twenty percent discount because you bring so much business to the inn."

"That sounds fair."

"I'm glad you think so," he said with mock gravity, earning himself a look.

He leaned over to set his wineglass on the table in front of the couch and drew a breath. He was about to take a major step, and he wasn't entirely sure how she would react.

"One of the guys I play basketball with a couple times a month just got a big promotion in his job. He'll be moving to Dallas in a few weeks. Some of us are getting together at another friend's house next Tuesday—a week from tonight—for a party in his honor."

"That sounds nice," she said, a little distracted by the cat, who had climbed into her lap and was sniffing her wine. She lifted her glass a little higher and set Fiona gently aside.

"So I thought maybe you could go with me. If you aren't busy that night."

It must have taken a moment for his words to sink in. When they did, she froze for a moment before asking, "You want me to go with you?"

"That's what I said."

"Like…a date?"

Okay, judging by her tone, he wasn't the only one who thought this was a big step. Still, he couldn't yet read anything in her expression except blank shock. "Exactly like a date."

"Oh, I don't—I don't think that's a very good idea."

His eyebrows beetled. "You have other plans that evening?"

She tucked her hair behind her ear in a nervous gesture. "No. I mean, I don't think so. I haven't checked my schedule, but we shouldn't go to a party together."

"Why not?"

Her loud sigh signaled impatience with his obtuseness. "Well, because. Even if your sisters aren't there, and even if they don't know your friends, it's still too likely that word would get back to them that you'd brought me as a date to the party. It's not like in Seattle, where the chances were slim that we'd be recognized."

"And yet, we were," he reminded her. He was getting a little irritated, but he warned himself to give her time to adjust to the idea before he started growling at her.

She waved a hand in dismissal. "Isabella never even heard your name. That's less likely this time."

"True. I would definitely tell my friends your name."

She looked agitated now, squirming on the couch until Fiona jumped down and walked away to find a more comfortable place to sit. "And you know what they would think."

"What would they think?" he asked her evenly.

"That we're a couple. Or at least that we're seeing each other."

"Alexis, we've been seeing each other—intimately—for seven months. I think it's time we stopped pretending otherwise, don't you?"

She set her wineglass on the table so hard it was a wonder it didn't shatter. And then she jumped to her feet and began to pace. He watched her in surprise, having seriously underestimated her response to his simple invitation.

"You think it's time," she repeated flatly. "Is that right?"

"Obviously, I wouldn't say anything without your consent. Which is why I asked you if you'd go with me to the party. Sort of easing into it."

"Easing into what?" she demanded, whirling to look at him.

He rose slowly. "Into going public. Seeing each other openly, without pretending we hardly know each other when we cross paths at the inn. We had our reasons when we started this thing. We figured it was no one else's business, and we didn't know if it would work out long enough to bother mentioning it to anyone else. It was great to have time to get to know each other without well-intentioned interference from family and friends. But we're past that point now, don't you think?"

"No. I don't think!"

He had to admit he was taken aback by her vehemence. "I don't get it, Alexis. What's going on here?"

He watched as she drew a deep breath, obviously struggling to regain her composure. She spoke more calmly then. "If we go public, as you say, everything will change. People—my mother, your sisters—will start expecting things from us. Asking us if we have plans for the future, that sort of thing. You said yourself it's been great with just the two of us. Do you really want to deal with that sort of outside pressure?"

He'd spent a lot of time asking himself those questions before inviting her to the party. Now he shrugged and said, "Maybe it *is* time we start thinking about the future. We're good together, Alexis. In bed and out. It's not such a stretch that we could stay together. Maybe even end up getting mar—"

She didn't even let him finish the word. "Stop! Just stop, okay?"

Squeezing the back of his neck with one hand, he glared at her. "I'm going to need a little clarification here. I don't know why you're freaking out like this."

"Because you're changing the rules," she shot back. "This is not what we agreed on. Everything's been going so well, and now you're trying to change it."

"You changed things when you invited me to join you in Seattle."

She winced. "Maybe that was a mistake. I thought we could have a good time, relax for a few days, then go back to the way we were after we came home."

His hand tightened at his nape as a jolt of pain shot through him. He dropped his arm, feeling himself stiffen. "Things change. Evolve. I thought we were moving forward in this relationship. Apparently I was wrong."

She threw up her hands, her face flushed, her eyes stormy behind her glasses. "We haven't had a relationship! We've had sex. An affair. That was what you said you wanted, and now out of the blue, you're saying something different. And you just expect me to go along with it?"

He didn't like hearing her describe it—their relationship—that way. "Look, I didn't mean— It's obvious I haven't handled this very well. If you don't want to go to the party, fine. We can talk."

"I think we've talked enough," she whispered, avoiding his eyes as she wrapped her arms around herself in a protective stance. "I think it's time to let it go."

"It?" he repeated coolly.

"Us."

She was ending it. Right here in her living room, without any warning, and all because he'd invited her to a party. He could hardly believe it was happening, but he'd be damned if he would beg. "If that's what you want."

She nodded, still speaking so quietly he could hardly hear her. "I think it's for the best. I hope you'll stand by your promise that this won't affect our working together. After all, of the two of us, I'm the one with the most to lose."

In one breath, he went from hurt to furious. "Is that right?"

She nodded again.

"Fine. You needn't worry that I'll say anything to affect your business reputation. I'll trust you not to take your clients away from the inn just because you're done with me. Kinley and Bonnie don't deserve that."

"I wouldn't—"

He was already moving toward the door. "You needn't worry that it will be awkward between us at the inn. Kinley would just as soon I stay out of client meetings, anyway. Tell her what you need, and I'll do my best to fill any reasonable requests to your clients' satisfaction."

"Logan—"

He didn't wait to hear more. He let himself out, closing the door sharply behind him, and stalked toward his truck. He should have known better, he thought savagely. Apparently, he hadn't learned the lessons his life had tried to teach him as well as he'd thought. He'd let himself care. Let himself hope. Let himself...

Love.

Damn it.

He really should have known better.

Chapter Eleven

For more than a week, Alexis vacillated between missing Logan so badly she ached with it and being utterly furious with him for ruining everything. Even after mentally replaying the scene a hundred times during the days since he'd stalked out of her house, she couldn't remember all the details of their conversation, how it had so quickly spiraled out of control. She did, however, remember that he'd started to imply that he was beginning to consider marriage as a potential future for them.

She freely admitted to herself now that she had panicked. To the point that she'd barely been articulate when she'd told him it was over. She knew she'd angered him with her rejection. Maybe she'd even hurt him, though probably it was more his pride than his heart that had taken the blow. He would get over it.

She wasn't entirely sure she would.

Had she really let herself go and fall in love with the man? Was she really that foolish, even though she'd spent most of her life believing that romantic lives didn't—couldn't—last?

Groaning, she planted her elbows on her desk and buried her face in her hands, unable to concentrate on the work surrounding her. Which was also his fault.

As she had many times before, she assured herself she'd done the right thing in ending it all before it got entirely out of hand. She'd hoped the end would be more amicable, less abrupt, but she'd always known it would come. Obviously, it had been time. If she hadn't taken that step, she and Logan could have gotten carried away with it all. She could have gone to his party with him. They could have had a great time. He'd have introduced her as his date, eventually as his girlfriend. They could have continued having great sex, having fun doing other things together, and their marriage-inclined friends and family would have started seeing them as a couple. Logan and Alexis. Alexis and Logan. Maybe they'd have even convinced themselves that they could make it work, despite the odds they knew so well.

That was exactly the way it had all taken place with Harry. Until it had crashed and burned.

If it hurt this badly breaking up with Logan now, how much more devastating would it have been if they'd ended up like her parents and their other spouses, like her brother and his two wives? When dissatisfaction set in, when novelty became habit, when bliss turned to bitterness? She'd seen it happen over and over. She'd lived it herself with her ex, though they'd never actually taken vows, thank goodness.

Of course, what she'd felt for Harry didn't come even close to the intensity of her feelings for Logan—and wasn't that even more reason to end it? For a time, she'd thought herself in love with Harry—but now she knew it had been mere infatuation compared to her feelings for Logan. In her observation, the hotter the passion, the faster it burned out. She just really didn't want to take the risk of having her heart in ashes around her feet.

"Hey, Alexis? You okay?"

Dropping her arms immediately, Alexis looked at her assistant with a too-bright smile. "Sure. Just wanting to beat my head against this desk over some of the requests Ellie Reid has come up with for her daughter's sweet sixteen party. Definitely a case of champagne tastes on a beer budget."

"Oh." Gretchen looked a little skeptical about the excuse. "You've been a little off your game this past week. I've wondered if you're coming down with something."

"I'm fine. Just a little tired."

"You should have taken a longer vacation in Seattle after the seminar."

"Trust me, that's just what I should *not* have done," Alexis replied flatly, a pang shooting through her with the reminder.

Gretchen's eyebrows rose, but she let it go. "Did you get a chance to sign that letter I left on your desk? If so, I'll get it in the mail."

"Yes, it's here."

The phone buzzed and Gretchen started to rush

toward her desk, but Alexis signaled that she'd take it, instead. She handed Gretchen the signed letter as she picked up the phone and answered professionally, identifying the company and herself.

"Hi, Alexis, it's Kinley."

Her pulse gave a little jump before she reminded herself that she and Kinley were still business collaborators. She doubted that this call had anything to do with Logan. "What can I do for you, Kinley?"

"I have the numbers for you on that catered retirement party you asked about. Just letting you know I'm emailing them to you now."

"Thank you, I'll watch for the email. I'm sure my clients will be satisfied with the estimate. You're always fair."

"Thanks, I hope you're right. We can always make adjustments as needed to bring costs down if they want."

"I'll discuss it with them. How are things at the inn?"

"Getting crazy as the summer creeps up on us, but I guess you know that feeling."

"Absolutely."

"We still haven't had a chance to have that lunch together. Are you free next week? Thursday, maybe?"

Was she really ready to have a chatty lunch with Logan's sister? Though she felt like a coward— again—she prevaricated, "I'll get back to you on that, if that's okay."

Kinley didn't seem to take offense. "Of course. Check your calendar and let me know."

"I will."

"So, how have you been, Alexis?"

A little surprised by the other woman's searching tone, Alexis answered brightly, "I'm fine, thank you. As you said, busy, but that's a good thing, right?"

"Of course. Although Bonnie and I are both about ready to strangle our brother."

"Oh?" She tried to speak with only casual interest. "Aren't your new protocols working out?"

"Oh, he's staying away from the clients, for the most part. He's just snapping our heads off. Not to mention his crew. I think his dog is the only one who hasn't had a chewing-out from him this past week."

"I see." She honestly couldn't think of anything else to say.

"Just in one of his moods, I guess."

"I guess so," she agreed lamely. "I'm sure it will get better soon."

"I certainly hope so. Let me know about lunch next week, okay?"

"Yes, I will. Thanks for calling."

With the call disconnected, Alexis tried once more to focus on work. Only to end up with her face in her hands again, a low groan escaping her throat.

It was almost dark on Thursday, more than a week after Logan had left Alexis's house, when his sister called him out on his behavior during the past nine days.

"When are you going to stop moping and do something?" Kinley demanded, glaring at him with her hands on her hips.

He straightened from the flower bed in which he'd just spread a new layer of mulch. His back ached a little from being bent over a shovel and his head hurt because he'd skipped lunch. Again. He'd worked such long hours during the past nine days that his left leg throbbed in protest. "What the hell do you mean, do something? Have you not seen all I've gotten done around here this week?"

"I don't mean do something about your job," she said with an impatient shake of her head. "You're working yourself to a frazzle around here. But that isn't helping, is it?"

He tossed the shovel across the top of his wheelbarrow. "I don't know what you're talking about."

"I'm talking about Alexis," Kinley shocked him by saying. "Are you just going to let her go without even trying to hang on to her?"

The silence stretched for a long time between them before he found the voice to reply. "Did she say something to you?"

"Of course not, you idiot. She's been as closemouthed as you are about whatever has gone on between you. But I'm your sister. And along with Bonnie, I know you better than probably anyone else alive. You've been seeing Alexis, haven't you?"

He wasn't going to lie to her. "I was," he admitted curtly. "It's over."

"Why?"

His first inclination was to snarl that it was none of her business. The only reason he didn't was because he knew Kinley wouldn't back down no matter how much he growled. So he said simply, "She's not interested."

"I don't believe that. I watched the two of you together when you thought I didn't notice. And I've heard her voice when she speaks of you, even though she didn't realize she was revealing anything. She's interested. So you must have screwed it up."

"All I did was ask her to a party," he snapped, indignant that his own sister automatically placed the blame on him. "How is that screwing up?"

"You must have asked her wrong."

He ripped off his work gloves and threw them in the wheelbarrow. "You don't understand."

"I understand that you're hurting," she said more quietly, placing a hand on his arm. "And I hate seeing that."

"I'll get over it."

"Do you really want to get over it? Or do you want to work it out with her?"

He exhaled slowly. "Doesn't matter what I want. Like I said, she's not interested."

"Maybe she's scared. Trust me, I know what that's like. I was terrified to fall in love with Dan and risk being left heartbroken again."

He thought of the night Kinley had come to his door in tears after a quarrel with Dan. His first instinct had been to find the guy who'd hurt his sister and pound him. Typical of Kinley that she yelled at him instead, when he was the one brooding.

"Maybe Alexis has been hurt before and is afraid to take another chance. You won't know until you ask her, will you? I know it takes a lot of courage to risk being shot down again," she added with a misty smile. "But will you ever forgive yourself if you give up this easily?"

He pushed a grubby hand through his hair. "Don't say anything to Alexis about any of this, will you?"

It was her turn to be indignant. "Of course not!

It's not my place to talk to her about something this personal."

He couldn't help but be wryly amused that she didn't see the irony of her words. She sure didn't mind getting into *his* personal business. "I'll think about it, Kinley," he said wearily. "But I don't want to talk about it again, okay?"

She patted his arm once more. "I won't bring it up again. Just know that I'm here whenever you want to talk."

"I know. And thanks." He leaned over to brush his lips briefly against his sister's cheek, then turned away to put up his tools.

Had he screwed up with Alexis? Pushing the wheelbarrow down the path to the cottage, he replayed the breakup with an attempt at objectivity. Maybe he'd come across as too pushy. Maybe she thought he was making decisions about their future without consulting her first, though he'd considered a simple invitation to a party as an opening to that important conversation. But maybe he'd gone about it all wrong.

Realizing that there had been little romance—even little emotion—in his airy comments to Alexis about moving forward with their relationship, he grimaced. Had he been too pragmatic? Hell, had he actually started to say they'd probably get married someday with the same casual tone he'd used to tell her about his friend's going-away party?

Would it make a difference if he told her how much he'd missed her during these past nine days? Would she care if she knew how much it hurt him to think it might really be over for good between them?

Thinking of the good times they shared, all the special moments between them, the way he felt when she was in his arms, he thought perhaps Kinley was right. He'd be a fool not to try at least one more time. And as terrifying as the idea was to him, he was going to have to bare himself to her—emotionally, this time.

Maybe he was just a glutton for punishment, he thought with a grim shake of his head. He could only imagine how he'd react if she shot him down again. He didn't like to think of himself as a coward, but he had to admit the thought of that potential scene made his gut clench.

He would talk to her tomorrow. Perhaps his sister had been right that he would never forgive himself if he didn't give it at least one more shot.

He unlocked his gate and pushed the wheelbarrow into the backyard, whistling for Ninja as he entered. Maybe a long walk would clear his head tonight, maybe help him get some rest before making his play tomorrow. If nothing else, it would keep him from spending an extra couple of hours moping alone in his living room.

Dropping the wheelbarrow handles, he brushed off his hands, then looked around for his dog. "Ninja? Let's go for a walk."

Odd. Usually the dog was all over him, bouncing around in excitement at the very mention of a walk. It was almost fully dark now and he narrowed his eyes to search the shadows for the black-and-brown dog. "Ninja? Hey, buddy, where are you?"

The silence in the yard made him nervous. He walked every inch of the fenced area, looking behind and beneath the storage shed, under bushes, under the chairs on the small back porch, picturing the dog hurt or sick. There was no sign of him.

Out of the corner of his eye, he thought he saw a wisp of white at the darkest back corner of the yard, but when he whipped his head around he didn't see anything moving. Still, he moved that way to look. He didn't find Ninja. What he found was a sizable hole beneath the fence, obviously dug by a dog's eager paws.

Torn between relief and aggravation, he grimaced. Great. Who knew what havoc the mischievous escapee was causing around the grounds? Kinley was going to strangle them both.

He tugged his phone out of his pocket and called Bonnie. "Just letting you know Ninja's gotten out of the yard. You might want to let your guests know that he's harmless before he pops out of a shadow and terrorizes someone."

"I'll send Paul out to help you look for him in case he decides to play hide-and-seek with you."

It wouldn't be the first time Ninja indulged in the game. "Thanks."

Leaving the yard, Logan headed toward the fountain, where Ninja usually hung out when he escaped. He whistled again, called the dog's name, mentioned "walk" and "treats." And was still met with no response.

Twenty minutes later, he and Paul had to admit that the dog didn't seem to be on the grounds. It was too dark to search the woods, though Logan walked a few yards down the trail, whistling and calling, before he gave up and returned to the inn.

Having joined the fruitless search, Bonnie looked

distressed. "Where could he be? He's never run off like this before. He always wants to be here with you."

"I don't know," Logan admitted, wishing he had a different answer. "I guess he started exploring and wandered farther than usual. I don't even know what time he got out. I haven't seen him since around noon."

"He'll come back, won't he?"

"Sure, he'll come back. Probably clawing at my door in the middle of the night."

"I hope so. I hope he's not hurt somewhere," Bonnie fretted, wringing her hands in front of her. "I really love that silly dog."

"He'll be fine, honey," Paul assured her, wrapping an arm around his petite wife's shoulders. Over her head, his eyes met Logan's, and Logan could tell that Paul, too, was concerned about the dog's atypical disappearance.

As for himself, he couldn't deny that his muscles were tense with worry about the dog. Ninja had just wandered up one day from who-knew-where. What if he'd gone walkabout again, even though Logan had thought the dog was happy here?

He didn't even want to think that his pet could be gone for good, not when he was still reeling from losing Alexis.

It was late Thursday evening by the time Alexis returned to her house from a family dinner to celebrate her stepfather's birthday. It had been a particularly exhausting ordeal, with her mother lecturing again on why Alexis should be married and procreating and Alexis doing her best to conceal her emotional turmoil. Suffice it to say, she was glad to be home.

She parked her car and opened the driver's door, which turned on the dome light above her. She caught a glimpse of her reflection in the rearview mirror as she reached for her purse. The face in the glass looked weary, melancholy. A far cry from the strong, independent woman she always considered herself to be.

She had always known falling in love would be a mistake. That she would be hurt. And yet, she thought with a sigh, she was the one who had walked away, not Logan.

She couldn't help thinking about the things Kinley had said on the phone yesterday. About how Logan was especially grumpy and moody lately. Was he missing her? Had she truly hurt him when she'd sent him away or was he just mad that she hadn't gone along with his agenda?

How hard had it been for him to take that step toward her? To make the decision to ask her out, even though he'd known being seen in public would raise eyebrows among their mutual acquaintances?

Had he really thought they were headed toward a serious relationship, despite the casually calculated beginning to their relationship? Had he really believed it might even lead to marriage, regardless of his wariness of that particular institution? Had he maybe believed that they'd be one of those rare couples who somehow made it all work out?

Dare she even hope that the odds just might be in their favor this time?

Maybe she should have talked to him about these questions, rather than freaking out, as he'd correctly labeled her reaction. She was becoming more and more convinced that she'd acted like an idiot, but now she wondered if it was too late to do anything about it. How could she face him now and try to have a rational conversation about their future? After she'd said all those terrible things?

She climbed out of the car and closed the door, darkening the interior again. An overhead pole lamp and her yellow porch light provided illumination for her to trudge safely toward her front door, though her mind was still filled with those unsettled questions about Logan. She jumped nearly a foot backward when a dark shape separated from the shadows beside her porch, growling.

Only when her heart began to beat again did she realize that the shape was Ninja and that the sound was his happy rumble-purr. Her knees went weak with relief, then stiffened again in anticipation. She looked around eagerly for Logan. Where was he?

"Logan?"

Ninja nudged against her, and she noted that he was panting a little. She rested a hand on his head. "Where's Logan?"

He couldn't be in her house; she'd never given him a key. Besides, Logan wouldn't leave his dog outside like this. But surely Ninja hadn't escaped the inn and come several miles here on his own?

She opened her door and he bounded inside with her, both of them greeted by her happy cat. She filled a bowl with water and set it on the kitchen floor, then watched as Ninja began to lap at it. She was becoming increasingly convinced that the dog was a runaway.

"Something tells me you've been a bad boy," she said to him even as she drew out her phone.

She hesitated a moment before dialing Logan's

number, but then swallowed hard and pushed the call button. He could be frantic about Ninja's whereabouts. He needed to know his dog was safe.

His phone rang several times, then the call was sent to his terse, no-nonsense voice mail. He didn't have a landline, only the cell, so she left a message. "Um, Logan? Hi, it's Alexis. I just found Ninja at my front door. I'm bringing him home now and I'll turn him over to Bonnie and Paul if you aren't there. I thought you might be worried about him."

Disconnecting the call, she pulled out her car keys again. "Okay, pal, let's go," she said to the dog, taking hold of his collar. "But you'd better prepare yourself. You're likely to be grounded without TV or video games for a week for this stunt."

The dog made a chuffing sound she'd have almost sworn was a laugh, but he accompanied her willingly enough outside to her car.

Logan prowled the grounds of the inn long after he'd sent Paul and Bonnie inside, futilely waiting for his dog to return, scanning the drive and the hiking path for any sign of the mutt. He'd tried settling in for the night in the cottage, but he couldn't relax. Nothing on TV could hold his interest, he couldn't read, couldn't just put up his feet and chill. Every time he tried, his eyes were drawn to the rug where Ninja would usually be lying at this point. So he could sit there brooding about Alexis and Ninja, or he could go out looking for the dog again. Of the two options, the latter had sounded more appealing, so here he was, restlessly pacing the paths. Maybe he'd go inside again soon. Not that he expected to get much sleep that night, for lots of reasons.

Would he be making his nightly rounds alone in the future? He sighed and pushed a hand through his hair, more miserable than he could remember being in a very long time.

He had just turned halfheartedly toward his home when he heard Ninja's funny growl behind him. Drawing a sharp breath of relief, he turned just as the dog bounded up to greet him joyously.

"Damn it, Ninja, you scared the hell out of me." Thinking there was no one to see his momentary display of weakness, he dropped to his knees to give the wiggling, whining dog a rough hug. "Do not do that again, you got it?"

He turned his head just in time to avoid being licked right on the mouth.

With a tired laugh, Logan pushed himself to his feet, wiping his face with the back of one hand. "Okay, we're going back—"

Something made him stop talking and look around. He was sure his eyes were playing tricks on him. "Alexis?"

For a moment, he thought he saw a pale figure standing behind her—one of his sisters, perhaps. But then she stepped forward into a pool of light and he saw that she was alone.

"I tried to call you," she said. "You didn't answer your phone."

Automatically he groped for his belt, then realized he must have left the phone in his living room when he'd gone in earlier. "Uh, left my phone inside. What are you doing here?"

"I brought Ninja home. I found him standing outside my house when I got home from having dinner with my mother and stepfather this evening."

"How the hell did he get to your house?" Logan asked in bewilderment.

"I think he walked. He was panting and very thirsty when I found him." She sounded as flabbergasted as he was by the dog's inexplicable behavior. "He didn't give me any trouble at all when I put him in the car and brought him back."

Squeezing the taut back of his neck, Logan stared down at his deceptively innocent-looking pet. "Have you lost your mind?"

Ninja yawned, then walked over to rub his head affectionately against Alexis's leg.

"Look, I'm sorry you had to go to this much trouble so late. You should have called Bonnie and had her send me to get him." Logan shook his head when Ninja strolled back to nuzzle his hand. "You're lucky she didn't call the dog collector," he said, though both he and Ninja knew Alexis would never do such a thing.

"It wasn't that much trouble."

He pushed his hands into his pockets and drew a deep breath. At almost the same time as Alexis, he blurted, "I was going to call you tomorrow."

"You were?" she asked, even as he said, "Wait. You were going to call me?"

He shook his head. "You go first."

He saw her moisten her lips. "I panicked."

"I know."

His blunt response took her aback for a moment, but then she surged on. "We had such a perfect time in Seattle. And your sisters are happy newlyweds and you're surrounded by weddings and honeymooners all the time. I was afraid you were suddenly seeing me through, you know, sort of a romantic haze. I guess you know, in my experience, that sort of emotion doesn't last. I've seen it over and over again, couples who fall madly in love—or lust—who declare each other perfect, and then later they can't even stand to look at each other. I can't live up to an idealistic image you might have formed of me. And when the magic wears off—"

He heard her swallow before she finished, "I suddenly realized how much you could hurt me. How much I've come to care for you. And...I panicked."

This night had become one disconcerting shock after another. "Let me get this straight. You decided I was being *too* romantic? Me?"

She had the grace to look sheepish. "Not in the typical, poetic sort of way, of course. That's not your style. But, well, all of a sudden you wanted to make our relationship public. And you...well, you hinted that maybe our relationship could lead to...you know."

She couldn't even say the word.

He could. "Marriage."

"Yes," she whispered, turning her face so that shadows fell across her features.

For a moment the only sound in the night-shrouded gardens was the whisper of a breeze through new spring leaves, the splash of water from the fountain, Ninja's happy panting by Logan's side. No one moved around them; the guests were closed inside the cozy inn, the lights glowing in the bedroom windows the only sign that anyone else was near. Alexis blocked out even those indications, keeping her attention focused solely on this momentous conversation with Logan. As far as she was concerned, they could have been the only two people around for miles.

Logan kept his voice low. "I don't idealize you, Alexis. Frankly, there are times when you're as much of a pain in the butt as my sisters."

She couldn't bring herself to smile. Her lower lip was caught between her teeth as she listened to him with her hands locked in front of her.

"I know you have flaws," he said, "but you should know I'm bored by perfection. And by those who pretend to be. I wouldn't change one thing about you."

He shoved his hands into his pockets, adding gruffly, "I know I'm no prize, myself. I'm grouchy and stubborn and inflexible—and those are just the things my loving sisters say about me. I've got scars—inside and out. And those scars put a lot of people off."

She was sincerely appalled when she released her lip to say with a slight gasp, "Surely you don't think your scars make you any less attractive to me?"

"You wouldn't be the first to back away because you heard me use the word *cancer,*" he said grimly. "That's a word that stays with you for a lifetime. Makes people wonder if you'll fall victim to it again, no matter what the annual medical exams show."

She took a step closer to him and looked straight into his eyes, her voice quiet but firm. "Come on, Logan, you know me better than that. I was shocked, of course, when you told me about your experiences. In all the months we've been seeing each other, you'd never mentioned it before and I had no idea. I'd like to hear more about it, because it's a part of who you are. I want to hear how you felt when you heard the diagnosis, what it was like to go through the treatments, how it affects you now. But the fact that you're a cancer survivor had nothing at all to do with my reluctance to get more deeply involved with you."

He blew out a breath. "I can answer those questions in just a few words. It sucked, treatment was hell and there's no reason to believe I'll ever have to go through it again, so it doesn't affect me at all now. We can talk more about it if you want to, but it's not something I dwell on. Much. My scars are all hidden by my jeans, and my limp isn't very noticeable, so the subject almost never comes up."

She took another step forward, bringing her to within inches of him. She laid a slightly unsteady hand on his chest, just over his heart, which she could feel beating rather hard against her palm.

"I don't think your leg was the only part of you left with scars," she said softly. "My childhood left me with quite a few hidden scars of my own. But I suppose mine are part of who I am today, just as your ordeals have forged you into the man you've become. 'Grouchy and stubborn and inflexible,'" she quoted, repeating the words with a shaky smile. "And I wouldn't change a thing about you, either."

He reached up to touch her face, his hand warm and work-roughened but oh so tender against her skin when he slowly removed her glasses. "That first night we were together, after we ran into each other at the coffee shop? It was the best experience of my life to that point," he murmured. "And it's only gotten better since. Every single time. You don't have to worry about the magic wearing off when it comes to the way I respond to you. I can't imagine ever getting enough of you. And I'm saying this as a cynical, very logical guy who never lets himself get swayed by all the romantic nonsense that goes on around this place."

She placed her other hand on his chest, leaning into him, her heart beating as rapidly as his now. "I'm still scared," she whispered frankly.

"Me, too," he said with a crooked smile. "We'll be scared together."

"Don't break my heart," she warned him, lifting her face to his.

His breath was warm against her lips when he murmured, "I'll give you mine to hold as collateral."

"That'll work," she said, just before he smothered the words beneath a kiss that went a long way toward healing the pain their split had caused them.

He lifted his head just long enough to say huskily, "I love you, Alexis. I have almost from the start, despite my efforts not to fall for you."

She smiled through a film of happy tears. "Despite all my best efforts, I love you, too. And suddenly I'm feeling really good about our odds."

"You should. My sisters swear there's magic in this place."

"I'm beginning to believe them," she said, and drew his mouth to hers again.

They broke apart a long time later when Ninja made a high-pitched whine from a few feet away. They turned together to see him holding a white flower delicately in his teeth, his happy smile gleaming in the soft artificial lighting of the garden. A ribbon of mist swirled around him, almost coalescing into a recognizable shape before slowly dissipating into the night.

Alexis looked quizzically at Logan, wondering if he'd seen what she had. His eyes were a bit wide when he looked back at her, but then he shook his head as if clearing away an errant flight of imagination. Obviously she had been imagining things. She couldn't even see all that clearly at that distance without her glasses.

Logan kissed her again and she pushed old tales and legends to the back of her mind. She was much more interested in the present, and the happy future she anticipated with Logan Carmichael.

The odds were definitely in their favor here on Bride Mountain.

* * * * *

A sneaky peek at next month...

Cherish™

ROMANCE TO MELT THE HEART EVERY TIME

My wish list for next month's titles...

In stores from 16th May 2014:

❑ Becoming the Prince's Wife – Rebecca Winters

❑ A Brevia Beginning – Michelle Major

❑ Taming Her Italian Boss – Fiona Harper

❑ Fortune's Prince – Allison Leigh

In stores from 6th June 2014:

❑ Nine Months to Change His Life – Marion Lennox

❑ The Single Dad's Second Chance – Brenda Harlen

❑ Summer with the Millionaire – Jessica Gilmore

❑ The SEAL's Baby – Laura Marie Altom

Available at WHSmith, Tesco, Asda, Eason, Amazon and Apple

Just can't wait?

0514/23

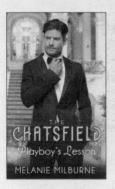

Join our *EXCLUSIVE* eBook club

FROM JUST £1.99 A MONTH!

Never miss a book again with our hassle-free eBook subscription.

★ Pick how many titles you want from each series with our flexible subscription

★ Your titles are delivered to your device on the first of every month

★ Zero risk, zero obligation!

There really is nothing standing in the way of you and your favourite books!

Start your eBook subscription today at www.millsandboon.co.uk/subscribe